The Secret Monster Within

Margaret McMillen

Outskirts Press, Inc.
Denver, Colorado

This is a work of fiction. The events and characters described herein are imaginary and are not intended to refer to specific places or living persons. The opinions expressed in this manuscript are solely the opinions of the author and do not represent the opinions or thoughts of the publisher. The author has represented and warranted full ownership and/or legal right to publish all the materials in this book.

The Secret Monster Within
All Rights Reserved.
Copyright © 2009 Margaret McMillen
V8.0

Cover Photo © 2009 JupiterImages Corporation. All rights reserved - used with permission.

This book may not be reproduced, transmitted, or stored in whole or in part by any means, including graphic, electronic, or mechanical without the express written consent of the publisher except in the case of brief quotations embodied in critical articles and reviews.

Outskirts Press, Inc.
http://www.outskirtspress.com

ISBN: 978-1-4327-2885-4

Outskirts Press and the "OP" logo are trademarks belonging to Outskirts Press, Inc.

PRINTED IN THE UNITED STATES OF AMERICA

In Appreciation

I'd like to offer a heart-felt thanks and all my love to my husband, Bob, who has been behind me all the way in the publication of this book.

Also, a special thank-you to Bill Lin for all the computer help, and his wife, Barb, for the many pics she took for the back cover.

And finally, a thank-you to Faye, my Outskirts Rep.

Chapter 1

Christy Donovan staggered to a stop, and while gasping for air, she shook her head in a silent form of surrender, as there was no use in denying it any longer. It was becoming quite clear that the time had come to cut back on her daily run by at least a half a mile, or possibly even a full one.

She managed a rueful smile as she spied a large boulder that had established itself on the side of the wooded path. Lately this had become her favorite resting spot, and she sat on it once again with a weary sigh. A water bottle from her backpack provided additional relief, and with closed eyes, she savored the sensation as the cool liquid caressed her parched throat.

It seemed only yesterday that she could run like a gazelle with no sign of effort, but now her heavy breathing was just another reminder that her thirtieth birthday was but one week away. She smiled at the inevitability of the aging process, and lifted her face to catch a bit of the summer breeze. She loved the sound of it as it whispered through the dense foliage.

Crack! What was that? Except for the murmur of the soft wind and the trill of the resident birds, there should be no other sound. One of the things she liked best about this trail was that it was away from the traffic and all the modern-day noise that filled her life at home. She knew this path like the back of her hand and this disconcerting noise was most unusual.

More cracking noise. Now her heart was beating doubly fast, as much from fear as from physical effort. She stood and scanned the area around her but saw nothing except the heavy brush and tall trees that had become her friends over the years.

Oh, for heaven's sake, she scolded herself, what are you afraid of? For a moment she had forgotten that the woods were full of deer. That's probably what it was, although she granted it would be most unusual since deer were notoriously shy during daylight hours. She shrugged her shoulders in bafflement and sat on the boulder once again since she still hadn't completely caught her breath.

The noisy rustle of the foliage behind her caused her to jump up once more. The movement was so quick, she barely realized what was happening until she felt the large, smooth hands surround her throat and close her windpipe.

"No!" She tried to scream, but only a whisper came from her gaping mouth. And then everything went black.

***

The Secret Monster Within

"I can't believe it!" Detective Halloway echoed everyone's reaction to the news. "I thought we were done with him."

"Well, some might think it's a copy-cat, but we know better, don't we? Everything fits, especially the one signature act that only we know." Amherst Police Chief Bernie Roper had been on the force for well over thirty-five years and his opinion held a lot of water in the minds of his cohorts. He was dark and swarthy, a man small in stature but big in the eyes of his fellow officers.

Detective Dan Halloway was the opposite in the extreme. His blonde hair and blue-eyed baby face didn't fit his six foot three inch stature, but looks be damned, like Roper, he was tough.

Being tough never got in the way of his feelings though. He felt a tug at his heartstrings as he viewed the photos once more.

"My God. Look at her. She was beautiful and just short of thirty years old, with a husband and a baby boy." His smooth brow crinkled in sympathy. "What causes people to do things like this?"

"I don't know if I'd give the fiend who did this the honor of including him with the rest of us people. He's The Monster he was so aptly named." Bernie's mouth curled in distaste.

"You can say that again."

***

"The Monster has been resurrected." Ken Lopez handed the newspaper to his wife of thirty-nine years. "But it seems he's now moved into our town of Amherst.

"What?" Maureen Lopez stared at the headlines and the blurred picture of the body. "Are they sure? He's been among the missing for at least seven years. Everyone thought he must be dead."

"Well, we certainly hoped so." Ken took the paper back from his wife and continued reading. "Good Lord. She wasn't even thirty. What's wrong with this creep?"

"As I remember it," Maureen paused in an effort to satisfy her memory, "the women he used to attack lived in Buffalo, and they were young and brunette, weren't they?"

"Well, it has been a long time, but I'm almost sure I remember it being that way." Ken paused in a concerted effort to recall the grim facts of the string of murders that had paralyzed the city just over seven years ago. "I'll tell you one thing though, Maureen. These serial murderers don't always care how young you are, so no more walking in the park alone. Please."

"Oh, Ken." She laughed and quickly dismissed his worry. "I'm over sixty years old, and I don't think any of his victims have been over thirty. He's got an MO, and it doesn't look like he's going to change it now."

"MO?" Ken scoffed at her. "Where did you learn to talk like that?"

"Hey. I watch television just like everyone else. I know what MO stands for …Modus Operandi. And we all know what his is, or at least was." Maureen nodded her head. "Yep. He likes them young, short and brunette. Don't have to worry about me, grandpa." She smiled as she patted his thigh.

"Well, you may be a grandma, but you're a pretty darn good looking one, kiddo. And I'm one gentleman who likes blondes." He smiled back at her and gave her a kiss on the end of her slender nose.

"Well, lucky for you, I don't." Maureen ruffled the full head of dark unruly locks her husband was forever trying to tame.

The Secret Monster Within

"Come here, woman. I may be in my sixties, but I ain't dead yet. Look what you've done. I need some fixin'."

Maureen laughed as she took his hand and headed for the bedroom.

***

"Hey, Dan. Have you been reading the papers?" Bernie leaned back in his office chair and turned the Buffalo News to page two.

"Nah. Why would I do that?" Dan raised his eyes skyward. Both the newspaper and all the local TV stations were filled with news of this latest killing, along with a large question mark. The police would not reveal specifics but it was reported that there were similarities that only the police were aware of, and it pinpointed the murder as the work of the man everyone knew as The Monster.

The headline shouted SAME MAN? The large question mark was followed by a string of little ones, and further reading revealed what they meant. Was this the same man who had terrorized the city seven years ago? If so, why such a long time between murders? Where had he been, in prison? Maybe sick? Maybe just tired of killing? And why did he choose the town of Amherst to resurface? The newspaper posed many questions, but had no answers.

"Well, at least let's hope that all this publicity will make The Monster's prospective victims more aware. They'd better not go out alone, and most certainly not on the bike paths or trails or parks." Bernie said this with the same intensity he would use with his own daughter if he had one.

He was frustrated by the lack of clues, the seemingly ease with which this monster killed and disappeared. They had to do something, but what? He wanted to personally reach out to all the vulnerable women in the area and tell them to be smart, prudent, and careful, but of course he couldn't. Local TV newscasts and The Buffalo News were the means used for passing this important message on to the public.

The warnings were becoming a mantra voiced by the parents of every young girl, and it seemed to be working. Now it was rare to see any woman walking alone, especially in the parks or on the trails.

Dan was only too happy to remind Bernie of the local news blitz and the resulting commonsense behavior of their local citizens.

"You're right. And thank God," Bernie added. "But don't forget, all it takes is one stupidly brave girl."

"Unfortunately, you're right on that one." Dan made a big show of crossing his fingers, the only thing left for them to do as of now.

***

"I must be crazy." Maureen Lopez always talked to her wheaten Cairn Terrier as though she were a child instead of a dog. "But you like this park so much, don't you, sweetie?" She pursed her lips in the form of a pouty kiss. The slight uphill walk and the soft breeze had turned her pale complexion to a rosy red.

"You realize I'm putting my life on the line for you, don't you?" Lady continued her exploration of the park's many shrubs with apparently no sign of the appreciation that her mistress was demanding. Instead, she squatted for a pee.

Maureen heard the rustle of the nearby bush and her heart jumped in her throat. Lady had just finished what she was doing and turned to growl at the unidentified intruder.

The Secret Monster Within

"Lady! Come!" Maureen bent in a failed attempt to pick up her dog and came almost face to face with a ground hog.

"Oh, for crying out loud. You scared me half to death." The scolding obviously didn't phase the ground hog one bit as he slowly turned and ambled back into the dense foliage.

Lady, however, shared none of the ground hog's calm demeanor. She barked and pulled on the leash in an attempt to reach the large rodent with such exuberance that Maureen had all she could do to maintain control.

Finally, she was able to gather her dog into her arms and turned to run. "Come on, Lady. Let's get out of here. That could have been something a lot worse. Maybe Daddy knew what he was talking about."

Her eyes smarted with tears as she realized what that *something worse* could have been.

Chapter 2

"Remind me not to have kids!" Jennifer Wilkins raised her eyes in a state of exasperation. "Why did I ever take this job?"

"There are some that are worse," the owner of Playground for Kids said with a great deal of patience. Melanie Longfellow had maintained her slim figure throughout the years, and her smooth complexion continued to belie her birth date. It was only the gray hair she refused to color that gave her age away.

Now she raised her eyebrows and looked at Jennifer over the rimless granny glasses she had perched on the end of her nose. "And if I remember correctly, you were having great difficulty in landing *any* position when I hired you two years ago. Have you forgotten?" She had an ordinary

The Secret Monster Within

face, but her warm smile turned it into a portrait of beauty. No one could resist that smile...well, almost no one.

"Not likely." Jennifer snorted, then returned to her charges which numbered twenty-three in all.

"Jimmy!" she shouted. "Don't touch that!" Quick as a whip, she reached four-year-old Jimmy Astor's side and relieved him of the scissors.

The tot's eyes welled with tears, and Jennifer was just as quick to give him a kiss and a hug. "It's all right, honey. We just don't want you to get hurt. OK?"

"OK." Jimmy's lips trembled.

Jennifer's tickle in the ribs turned the tide and he couldn't resist a giggle.

"You're one tough broad, but you're still my favorite employee." Mrs. Longfellow laughed at their shared joke since both were aware that Jen was Melanie Longfellow's only employee.

"Yeah." Jennifer made as fierce a face as possible, then broke out in a grin.

Four years of college, with a major in education and a minor in psychology, had netted her a job in a childcare program that was pretty much that of a glorified baby sitter. This certainly didn't fit her plans to become an elementary school teacher, but after graduating, she was to find that for every teaching vacancy in Buffalo and its surrounding suburbs, there were hundreds of applicants. The competition proved to be too much, and even though she had interviewed for teaching positions in Buffalo and a number of local towns, there were no callbacks.

Times were tough all over, but the city of Buffalo, New York, was one of the hardest hit by the latest recession. Steel plants were closing right and left, and smaller companies were being swallowed in their wake. As it was, Jen was happy to get any form of employment.

Margaret McMillen

As a matter of fact, even though she wouldn't admit it to anyone else, especially her mother, she loved her job. Maybe it was because she was an only child and had missed all those years of a sister or brother relationship. Or maybe it was just born in her. She didn't know. All she knew was that somewhere deep inside of her, there was a love for children that couldn't be ignored, and it seemed natural that children would love her back. This, of course, would explain her popularity among all of her charges at Playground for Kids.

The building was located on a busy street, but the surrounding fence and locked gate allowed the children to safely play on the jungle gym and swing sets they so loved during clement weather. The interior consisted of one large room with an adjoining cloakroom and two lavatories, one bearing the silhouette of a little girl and the other, a little boy.

Of course, there was a piano, and Jen had taken enough piano lessons that she had no trouble playing the simple tunes the kids loved to sing. And if she wasn't available, Mrs. Longfellow could be counted on to fill in, although Mrs. Longfellow had to admit she could neither play or sing as well as young Jen did. Luckily, the children didn't seem to care which of their caretakers led them in this, one of their favorite activities.

There were all manners of art supplies, including easels, paints and brushes, crayons, coloring books, and construction paper by the reams. The walls of the main room were adorned with the artwork of each child, including the youngest who, though not proficient in the field of art, still produced modern masterpieces with hand paints. In addition, there were games and balls and storybooks by the dozen. Little home appliances occupied one corner of the room and had accompanying miniature tables and chairs

The Secret Monster Within

where the children loved to play house with their dolls.

To instill a sense of responsibility, it was the older children's duty to clean and feed the three bowls of goldfish and two cages of live canaries. And after all the play and work was done, there were mats the children used for naps, each having their owner's name taped on it. It seemed there was nothing lacking to stimulate and educate these little ones under Jen's and Mrs. Longfellow's care.

Jennifer had to admit that even though this job wasn't what she had envisioned when she took elementary and psychology at college, strangely enough, it suited her to a Tee.

Not everyone felt that way however.

***

"Well, your career choice certainly isn't what we hoped for," her mother was only too happy to remind her again…and again.

"Hey, mom. I'm doing the best I can. It's a full time job with some benefits. I know the pay stinks, and there certainly isn't much glory in watching a bunch of kids, but…." Her voice trailed off because there was no *but*.

"Mrs. Longfellow likes me. And so do the kids," she added weakly.

"I know they do, honey." Her mother raised her hands in surrender and shook her head as she apologized. "I'm sorry. You're right. You've got a job and you do it well. You deserve kudos for that." She tipped her head and shrugged. "I just wish you could have gotten a teaching job."

"Me too," Jen said, with a returning what-can-you-do-about-it shrug. She knew this is what her mother wanted to hear. "And by the way," she couldn't resist adding with a smirk, "who else do I know that didn't get one?"

Vanessa Wilkins laughed. "Like mother, like daughter, huh? Two of a kind."

"Come here and let me comb your hair." Vanessa motioned for her daughter to sit on the kitchen chair in front of her.

Jennifer obediently sat where directed with a sorry look upon her face. "Look what I get for taking after you, Mom. I'm short and tiny and worse yet, look at this mess of hair." Jen pulled her too curly hair out with both fists in an effort to straighten it. "Why did I have to get your frizzy mop instead of Dad's?" Jen had always been jealous of her father's silky dark brown hair.

"Luck of the draw." Vanessa laughed. "And it's not frizzy. It's a mass of soft curls that you don't have to do anything with. Do you know how many girls would give their right arm to have this?" She caressed the jet-black locks and twirled a few around her finger.

***

Jennifer Wilkins came from a middle class family who lived in a middle class house. And, if the truth were stretched a bit, you could say she had done middling well in grades kindergarten through college. In fact, a great deal of her life could be classified as middling, but that would not include the love she received from her parents.

Vanessa and Troy Wilkins met while in college and it was the classic love-at-first-sight syndrome. Both were mature beyond their years so they had wisely decided not to marry until they had graduated, and everything went as planned. Well, almost.

They graduated in May, and were married in June. Neither was able to get a position in the field in which they had

The Secret Monster Within

received their degree, but they had swallowed their pride and took what was available at the time. Troy started off by working in a warehouse.

"A warehouse!" his parents exclaimed with disgust. "Why did we send you to college to get a business degree?" They did nothing to hide their feelings of annoyance.

It hurt but he persevered, and through hard work, he rose through the ranks to that of Manager, the position he held today. And his parents had willingly eaten crow.

Vanessa had not been lacking in her attempts to help get them off the ground either. Although there were no teaching assignments available after she graduated, she was able to obtain a job in the humanities field. That was just fine with her, as her plan was simply to work until her dream of becoming a mother came true. Luckily, she had no idea how long that would prove to be.

For some reason, unfathomable to both her and her husband, she had been unable to conceive. All the tests proved each partner to be fertile and there were no signs of malformation of either of their childbearing organs. The doctor's advice was always the same: Just keep trying.

"Do you think it's because I'm so tiny?" she asked her husband, and then her doctor.

"Of course not," they both assured her.

"Just keep trying."

Just keep trying. Just keep trying. The sex that had once been wondrous was now becoming a chore, and neither approached it with the same zest they used to feel.

One evening, after they had finished their dutiful act of procreation, Vanessa stared into the black night, feeling empty and depressed. Would now be a good time to ask a question she had been contemplating for some time now? She had no idea how Troy would take it. Would he be hurt? Would he be mad? Would she be casting an aspersion on his manliness?

"Troy," she said, and was surprised at how querulous her voice sounded, "do you think it's time for us to start thinking about adopting?"

The question hung in the air, and the silence was deafening. Vanessa slowly turned her head to look at her husband. The opened bedroom door admitted just enough of the hallway's soft light that she was able see his profile. He was staring wide-eyed at the ceiling, looking surprised, as if the idea had never occurred to him.

Oh, God. What have I done, she wondered? Vanessa's heart was racing with apprehension and she could feel her throat closing up. Please, Troy, say something! Answer me!

Troy turned to look at her and smiled as he took her hand. "You know, honey, that may not be a bad idea."

All of a sudden, a whole world of possibilities opened up, and Vanessa was giddy with delight.

"Troy! Really?"

"Yes, honey. Really." He laughed as he felt a load lifted from his shoulders.

Vanessa turned to kiss him, and the same fire they used to feel was back.

They had barely started looking into adoption procedures when they discovered that Vanessa was pregnant with Jennifer, who would prove to be their only child.

Chapter 3

"The Monster's returned."

"Oh, no." Vanessa Wilkins' fifty-two-year-old brow creased into a worried frown as she accepted the evening newspaper from her husband.

She had read but a few lines when her face went white. "Troy. It happened right here in *our* town. When he did that rash of them years ago, they were all in Buffalo."

Amherst was a suburb of Buffalo but, somehow, whatever happened in the city always seemed so far away. This was a first for Amherst. A young woman by the name of Christy Donovan had been murdered in their town, one of the widely advertised safest towns in America.

"This can't be happening." Vanessa stared at her husband as if he could make it go away.

"It's scary," Troy said. "And now I wish Jen were back here, living with us." Troy was of medium height, close to five nine, and very muscular. It had been that rock-hard body that had first attracted Vanessa Steven's attention so long ago, and it hadn't changed a bit over the years. Rock hard or not, he had a soft heart, and Vanessa could see him clenching his jaw. She knew he was more nervous than he cared to show.

"Oh, Troy." Vanessa's hazel eyes filled with tears that overflowed as she thought of her daughter's vulnerability. "I can't help but think of how long Jennifer wanted to move out on her own, and how long we resisted because we didn't want to lose her. She may not act as mature as we'd like, but you've got to admit, she's got a heart of gold." She closed her eyes in gratitude for having such a thoughtful daughter.

"And wouldn't you know it?" Vanessa shook her head in desperate despair. "We finally gave in, so she's moved out on her own, and it's at the same time this maniac who kills short brunettes has been resurrected. Oh Troy, I'm so afraid for her. What should we do?" Vanessa heard the whine in her voice, and hated it.

"I don't know, honey," Troy said, as he shrugged in an obvious state of bewilderment.

"I'm going to call her," Vanessa said with staid determination. "We've got her empty bedroom here." Vanessa rose to get the phone.

There was no answer.

She turned to her husband with a blank look. "Where is she?" Again her eyes sparkled with crystal droplets.

"Vanessa, relax. She's probably out with Vince, or," Troy threw his hands up, "with her girlfriends. Just because she's not home doesn't mean she's been murdered. She must have forgotten her cell. Here, let's call Donna and

The Secret Monster Within

Rob. Maybe they'll know where she is." Troy's hands shook as he dialed the number of Jen's landlords. The phone was answered on the second ring.

"Donna. How are you doing? This is Troy. We were just wondering if you knew where Jen was?" He was working hard at trying to sound nonchalant without much success.

"Oh, hi, Troy. Yeah, I think she went out with Vince tonight. Shall I have her call you if she gets in on time?"

"That would be great. We'd appreciate it. Thanks a lot." He was spitting the words out like bullets from a machine gun.

"You're welcome." It had taken but a moment for Donna to realize why he was calling. "You're reading the newspaper, aren't you? Scary, huh?" She sensed right away that he needed reassuring. "We've told Jen not to go out alone and she has promised us she won't."

Troy knew that Donna and Rob Mitchell were only four years older than Jen, but that was a fact that proved difficult to remember since they seemed so much more mature than their twenty-five-year-old daughter. They had reached a decidedly different status in life.

And now Donna's calm reassurance over the phone helped subdue his nervousness. "Well, I feel better now," he said with a heavy sigh. "Thanks, Donna."

"No problem, Troy. Rob and I will keep an eye on your little girl. Promise."

After each saying their mutual goodbye, Troy gently placed the phone onto its cradle, and turned to his wife. "See? No need to worry, Mommy. Jen is out with Vince, and Donna assures me that she and Rob have received a promise from her that she won't go out alone." Troy put his arms around his wife and pressed her to him as an added means of reassurance.

Margaret McMillen

***

Donna closed her cell phone and shook her head as she felt the added weight of an unexpected responsibility rest on her shoulders. Little did she and Rob know when they took on the job of lessors that they would be called upon to serve as surrogate parents to their tenants, and most especially to Jen Wilkens, the proverbial Alice in Wonderland who just didn't want to grow up.

Rob Mitchell chuckled as Donna related the phone message to him. "Someday, when we have kids, we'll understand how they feel," he told her, and she was quick to agree. Just a couple more years they had promised each other. Now she returned his smile and blew him a kiss from across the room. Their finding each other had been a miracle of sorts.

Rob was so tall that he had given up hope of ever finding someone who would want to share a life with him. Luckily he was well built, and at six foot eight inches, he became known among his acquaintances as the gentle giant. Lots of brawn, but a pussycat at heart. He stoically took the ribbing that all of his friends, and even some strangers, felt compelled to offer, so no one knew how much it hurt. Some remarks were clever, but most were run-of-the-mill, more often than not about the crick in their necks that came as a result of looking up at him. OK. That one was getting pretty old.

His brawn was matched with a handsome face. His eyes were a robin-egg blue, his nose was chiseled straight, and he had a soft generous mouth. A head of wavy light brown hair, which he wore at a medium length, framed these features. But this height thing had so warped his opinion about himself that he found it difficult to accept anyone's compliment.

The Secret Monster Within

His mother and father had both been tall, but nothing like this. "What's wrong with being 6'3" or 4?" he would ask his reflection time and time again, as he stooped to glare into the mirror. And then he would snarl at the reflected image because it had no answer.

Of course he had tried dating, but he dwarfed whomever he was with, and as the recipients of tongue-in-cheek laughter, his dates would refuse a second request. It seemed he was doomed to be a very tall and very lonely man for the rest of his life.

He was fast becoming a recluse and he was only twenty-one. Again he refused his friends' requests that he accompany them to The Darwin, a local club where the music was hot and the food was good. How he longed to do all these normal, natural things his friends did, but wherever he went, he knew he would become the object of attention, and often ridicule. It was easier to stay at home and watch TV.

But this time, Glen Grayson would not hear of it. "Come on, Rob." Glen had been his friend from childhood, back when they were both almost the same height. "Why do you put yourself down? Stand up and be proud of who you are. There are a lot of guys out there who would give anything to be as tall as you are. And you're better looking than any of us," he added with a grin. If it hadn't been Glen, Rob would never have given in.

But he did, and it was providence. He saw her the minute she walked through the door. She towered over all those around her, but she stood tall and proudly surveyed the night club scene. It was then their eyes met, and it was instant electricity. Volts of it ran though his body, and he just knew sparks were shooting from his eyes. They had to be.

He rose as if in a trance and walked over to where she stood by the door. "Hi," he said. She smiled and every cell in his body was alive and dancing.

"Looks like we have something in common," she said with a laugh.

"I guess so," he was quick to agree. She couldn't have been more than six or seven inches shorter than he was, and she was wearing flats!

She put her hand out and told him her name was Donna Svenson. Neither Glen nor any of his friends saw much of him for the remainder of the evening. He was totally enamored with this lovely lady. Her fresh Swedish blonde looks melted his heart, and—and—she was almost as tall as he was. *She was almost as tall as he was.* This was a miracle.

That was the first day of the rest of his life. No more holing up in his apartment, watching TV. He had a girl, and the two of them became the object of adoration wherever they went. Both so tall, so good-looking, and so much in love. What could be better?

Nothing, except making it permanent. They married, worked hard, bought a home, and were now landlords to young adults.

Upon purchasing their house, they had wisely agreed that the best way to ensure the continued affordability of it was by renting the two upstairs' bedrooms, which at this point in their lives were superfluous. The two on the first floor served them well enough, one being used as a master bedroom and the other as an office/hobby room.

And it had worked out beautifully. Gerri Meisner, a very mature and cerebral college student, had been one of their tenants for almost three years now, but Joyce Slater, their other tenant, had just recently graduated and was returning to her home in Connecticut. An ad had been placed in the Buffalo News and Jennifer Wilkins was the first to answer it. Both Troy and Vanessa had accompanied their daughter on her interview with the Mitchells.

The Secret Monster Within

Rob sold drugs. "No," he chuckled, "not *that* kind. Pharmaceutical," he went on to explain to Jen and the senior Wilkins. It wasn't easy at first, he admitted, but now with almost four years' experience under his belt, he was doing just fine. So fine, in fact, Donna no longer had to work, and that was a gift because now she had the time to do what she truly loved to do, which was to create works of art via oils and pastels. All of this information had been offered so the Wilkins might feel less worried about letting their daughter rent a room from them, and it worked.

After meeting with the Mitchells, their marked maturity had calmed Vanessa's and Troy's fears about letting their daughter go out on her own. And they were equally pleased after meeting Gerri Meisner, since there were actually three people they liked and trusted who would be living in the same house as their daughter.

Chapter 4

"Haven't you had enough to drink?" Vince Marotti reached for the glass Jen was tilting for the last drop.

"Since when did you become my father?" Jen pulled the glass away from him and laughed as she poured herself another one.

"I may not be your father, but I know when you've had too much. And you've had too much."

"Hey. I left my parent's home. I don't need another father. Got it?"

"I got it. When are you going to get it?" Vince's tone was developing a harder edge.

He shook his head and said more softly, "Give me that drink, Jen. You'll be sick."

The Secret Monster Within

"You know what? I am sick." Jen raised the glass and swallowed half the drink. "I'm sick of listening to you trying to boss me around."

"What's the matter with you, Jen? You know I love you. I just want what's best for you."

"Well, maybe you are what's best for me, and then again, maybe you aren't." Jennifer rose and staggered toward the door of his apartment.

"Where do you think you're going? You haven't got a car and no way to get anywhere without me." Vince blocked her means of exit.

"Get out of my way." Jen's words were slurred.

"Do you know who's out there? A serial killer who likes pretty young girls with dark hair." Vince put his arms around her shoulder and led her back into the room. "Just sit and have your drink if that's what you want. I'll make some coffee and then we can talk more. OK?"

Jen realized the futility of trying to get by her boyfriend. She shrugged in a means of surrender and told him that sounded good. She flopped on the sofa again.

"I'll be right back." Vince kissed her cheek, and took her drink in a sly move from the side table.

"OK." It looked as if Jen was about to fall asleep.

Vince hurried as fast as he could. He wanted to get some coffee and food served before she became any more inebriated. "I'll be out soon," he called, but received no response. Well, sleep might be the best thing. Nevertheless, he carried the tray into the living room as soon as the coffee finished dripping. Three cups didn't take that long.

"Here you go, honey." He stared at the empty couch and saw that the front door was ajar.

"Jen!"

He dropped the tray on the coffee table and ran out the open door.

"Jen!"

She didn't have keys to his car, so she had to be walking somewhere. She couldn't have gone far despite all her trophies for track. The coffee hadn't taken that long. Had it?

"Jennifer!" He was frantic and he looked it. A lonely hobo shied away from him in apparent fear.

"Did you see a pretty girl with black hair pass by?" It was late at night and Vince would not normally talk with the ragged person he now faced, but the streets were empty and he was his only chance. "Which way did she go?"

"I don't know what you're talking about. I didn't see anyone." The man in rags turned to go.

"Wait. Please. If you saw her, tell me. I'll give you some money." Vince fumbled through his pockets. "I don't have much. Here. Five Dollars." He offered the money. "That's all I've got. Did you see her?"

"Hey. I'd like to take your money, but I didn't see her. Honest." Even the man in rags didn't know where this streak of valor came from. "Sorry, buddy."

Vince looked up and down the empty streets. His apartment building was located just inside the Buffalo city-limits on a six-way intersection, and he had no idea which way to turn. "Keep an eye open for her, will you?" Vince handed the five dollars to the homeless man and turned to go into his apartment building.

"Thanks, man. I'll keep my eye open for her. I promise." The man in rags pocketed the money and walked away.

***

Donna and Rob were awakened from a deep sleep. The front door banged, and the thumping noise of heavy foot-

The Secret Monster Within

falls going up the stairs sounded as though they were being made with lead feet. Donna glanced at the clock on her nightstand and moaned when she saw it was 4:30 AM.

"That must be Jennifer," she whispered to an awakening Rob.

"At four thirty in the morning? What has she been doing since she left Vince? And why did he have to call and load his problem on our backs?" Rob looked at his watch in an effort to see if the ridiculous hour showing on the clock was right. It was.

"I don't know, but she's home now. Let's go back to sleep. I didn't know when we took her on as a tenant that we were really adopting a child. Damn." Donna punched her pillow and rolled over with a vengeance. "We'll talk to her in the morning."

"Sounds good to me." Rob was quick to agree.

"Jen." Donna peeked over her morning break coffee at the apparition that had just shuffled into the kitchen. "Up bright and early, eh?"

Jen's flannel robe and fuzzy slippers didn't fit the season. She looked at the wall clock through what seemed to be a film of gauze and thought she saw the hands at eleven o'clock.

"Well, at least I'm recognizable. You sure my head isn't ten feet wide?"

"I know that feeling only too well. Actually," Donna tipped her head at Rob, "we both do, don't we, hon?"

"Yep. Been there, done that. No more, thank you."

Donna and Rob, at twenty-nine, were sounding more and more like Jen's parents.

"Ooooo." Jen pressed her fingers to her forehead. "That hurts."

"Here, let me get you some coffee. Dry toast will help too."

"Thanks, Donna. I promise I won't do this again. I'm sorry." She groaned as she sat with a heavy thud on the wooden kitchen chair.

"We all have to learn the hard way. Welcome to the world of the living," Donna said with an all-knowing smile.

"This is the world of the living?" Jen held her fuzzy head in both of her hands.

The coffee tasted good, and the toast seemed to settle her stomach. "You two have been just great."

"Well, we like you, Jen, and we don't want anything to happen to you. You've got to start taking better care of yourself." Now Rob was sounding even more like her father.

In order to stem the flow, Jen quickly admitted her wrongdoing and swore she wouldn't do it again. "Honest," she averred with raised hand.

"Call Vince as soon as you can. He's been calling all morning." More suggestions from daddy dearest.

"Will do," Jen promised with a weak smile

***

"How did you get home?" Vince Morotti was angry, and rightfully so.

"How do you think? I walked." Jen regretted her flip answer as soon as she said it.

"Walked? How many miles is that? And it was in the middle of the night!"

The phone crackled with static. She didn't need phone-a-vision to know exactly what he was doing and what he looked like.

At five ten, he towered over her five foot. And like so many young Italian men, he was sexy and handsome. It wasn't fair that she had to fight to get her white skin to

The Secret Monster Within

show the tiniest bit of tan, while his was just naturally a beautiful bronze, no sun needed. And when she would lather mascara on the thin lashes that framed her blue eyes, she would seethe with jealousy thinking about his big brown eyes and the long thick lashes he had been born with. "It isn't fair!" she would tell him, and in response, he would laugh, then kiss her and tell her how beautiful she was.

No such niceties now though. She could hear the fierce scowl in his voice, and knew the anger he felt towards her foolish behavior had furrowed his brow and was spoiling the look she loved so much. She could envision those large brown eyes shooting fire, and his soft lips were probably stretched into a thin line of distaste.

"Look, Vince, I know I was wrong. I was just fed up with being treated like a baby."

"Yeah? Well, what you did was very childish... *and* very dangerous. You know that, don't you?"

Here it was again, the inquisition. "Yes, I know it. I'm sorry. Really I am."

The tenor of his voice changed remarkably. "You know if I didn't love you so much, I wouldn't care what happened to you. But I do. I love you with all my heart, and I do care what happens to you."

"Oh, Vince, I know you do. And I love you too, just as much." Jen was surprised at how strongly she felt this. "I'm sorry. I'll see you tonight. OK?"

"Can't wait." Vince threw her a kiss over the phone.

"Got it," Jen told him, and blew him one back.

Chapter 5

Bernie Roper stared at the pile of photos he had stretched out on the long table, all of them beautiful young women who were now dead, thanks to this creature that lived among them. This latest victim, Christy Donovan, came close to bringing tears to his eyes. It could have been his daughter if he and Ella had been able to have children. She looked so much like Ella did when he first met her.

His eyes went dreamy as he recalled that day so long ago. It was summer, just like now, and he and his buddies had taken advantage of the beautiful weather to go to Sherkston, a quarry that had filled with water and was everyone's favorite swimming spot. It was just over the Niagara River and less than a half-hour's drive into Canada. Bernie had finished his first year at the local Erie Commu-

The Secret Monster Within

nity College and was on summer break, as were most of his buddies, even those who had opted for college out-of-state. Hey, where else to go? Everyone wanted to relive those "wild and crazy days of their youth" as they jokingly referred to their high school years.

He and his friends had finished swimming the mile-wide quarry once over and back again, and came out gasping for air. They walked the man-made beach to where their towels lay.

"Hey, Bernie, not as young as you used to be?" You could always count on his lifelong buddy, Jeffrey Carson, to be there when you needed him.

"Look who's talking. I didn't see you crossing it even once." Bernie laughed as he snapped his towel at his buddy's legs.

"Whoa." Jeff put his arms up in a mock mode of surrender. "Here. Have something to drink." Jeff gave him a peace offering.

"Thanks. I need one." Bernie took the proffered can of soda pop and gulped it down all at once. This resulted in a loud belch, which of course elicited gales of laughter from all his friends.

It was then that he saw her for the first time. She appeared like a goddess emerging from the sea. Long dark auburn ringlets caressed her back, and she shook them to discard the excess water. The white two-piece bathing suit served to accent her mahogany tan even more. Her eyes were huge in size, chocolate brown in color, and were surrounded by ridiculously long dark lashes. She was short but had a body to die for. And the best, the very best, was her smile. It was dazzling, and he was a goner the minute he laid eyes on her.

"That's my future wife," he told his friends in a tone of wonder.

"Yeah. Lots of luck, Bernie."

Bernie had to admit later that luck is what he needed. He introduced himself and she was polite, but seemingly uninterested. Fortuitously, it was then that his friend, Johnny Rae, happened to return from the refreshment stand.

"Ella." Johnny waved to her.

"Well, look who's here. How are you doing, Johnny?" The sea goddess walked over to give him a hug.

"Fine, thanks." His grin went from ear to ear. "Hey, I want you to meet some of my buddies."

Bernie had never given his looks much thought. I am what I am, like me or not. This had been his creed, and up to this moment, a solid base as to whom he was. But now as he stood before this sea goddess, he wished for so many things that he could never be. Why aren't I taller? Why don't I have massive muscles? Why is my nose so big? Why is my hair so straight? Why aren't I as good-looking as she is beautiful? Why can't I be someone she would want as much as I want her?

He and his friends were introduced to the most beautiful woman he had ever seen in his entire life, and that totaled nineteen years and seven months. Bernie, the glib one, the one with the golden tongue, lost it. He mumbled and stammered so much, Jeff threatened to slap him to bring him out of it. This was much to the amusement of all his friends.

Ella was much more forgiving. She smiled and offered her hand in greeting and told him how happy she was to make his acquaintance.

Bernie lived up to his promise when Ella and he were married two years later. And that was the beginning of twenty-six years of bliss.

Bernie had finished obtaining his college degree and

The Secret Monster Within

had gone through all the physical and mental requirements to become a policeman, so it was a red-letter day when he became a member of the Amherst Police Department. Ella always told him how proud she was of him and his profession, and had even suggested he wear his new uniform on their wedding day. His parents had talked him out of it and that was something he would later regret.

Although there were to be no children, no couple could have been happier or more in love then these two. And that's what made it all the more a nightmare when Ella discovered a lump in her right breast while doing a self-exam in the shower.

It was cold and rainy, a typical late March day when winter showed tiny signs of surrendering to spring. Ella and Bernie barely noticed as they trudged through the melting slush and approached the front door of Roswell, one of America's leading cancer hospitals that was conveniently located in downtown Buffalo. After a biopsy and the resulting bad news, Ella was forced to face her own mortality at the age of forty-seven.

They fought the valiant fight as a team and did anything and everything the doctors recommended, but the big C was not to be vanquished.

Life was unfair, and he railed against her eminent fate, and beat his fists into hard objects. He screamed against the lengthening shadow of death that was overwhelming them, and he cried, but nothing would frighten it away. Death won, and Bernie was a widower at the age of forty-nine.

Her death had not been kind. It was a long drawn-out affair, the type you wish upon someone who personifies the ultimate in evil, certainly not for one who was the sweetest, most loving of human beings like his Ella.

He lost track of time after Ella's death, and went through a period of mourning he remembered only as a gray fog. He slept, he ate, he did all the things a person has to do to continue living, but he was numb. He barely remembered seeing friends, though they had all gathered round him to lend their support. He couldn't tell you how well he performed at work. Obviously well enough to keep his job, but again, it was lost in a misty haze.

That was years ago. Everyone knew they had to give him time to grieve, but eventually each adapted the mantle of a psychiatrist and decided it was time for him to be brought out of his funk. They introduced him to one lovely girl after another, and he was polite, but resisted stoically. Why couldn't they see that no one could compare to his beloved? It took a while, but his friends finally got the message. "He'll come out of it in his own time," they decided, and they quit trying.

They were wrong, of course. He never really did come out of it. Even now, after all these years, he still lived in the same house he and Ella had bought shortly after they were married, the difference now being there was no lovely lady to share it with, only a German Shepherd he called Gus, and a twenty-pound cat named Attila.

Bernie couldn't take his eyes off the glossy photo of the latest victim.

"Why did you have to die?"

He didn't know if he was talking to the girl in the photo or the phantom one in his memory.

Chapter 6

Oh, how he loved the outdoors, especially at dawn. He saw the red glow on the eastern horizon and knew it would be another beautiful day. The sky's gray shroud may fool some, but he knew it would soon change into a blue satin gown.

He loved colors, and his favorites were those of nature. Buffalo was universally known as a blue-collar area, and that would illicit pictures of factories, smoke stacks, soot and grime, and of course, to some extent that was correct. But what wasn't publicized was the abundance of greenery that was almost blinding to those not used to it. No one had bothered to tell the world that Buffalo and its surrounding areas hosted more trees and parks than almost any other city in America. In fact, Buffalo was not only known as

Margaret McMillen

The City Of Good Neighbors, it was also known as the City Of Trees. The vast array of elm, maple, locusts, oak, poplars, willows, and on and on, was something to brag about. And so why didn't *they*...those politicians who laughed at all the jokes laid upon their doorstep? They promoted Buffalo's bad image by remaining silent. And there were so many good things that could be said about his hometown, like the vast trove of world-renowned architecture, the nearby rivers and lakes, and its many parks. So many outstandingly good things, he mused. But then, of course, we would lose our only claim to notoriety, wouldn't we? Maybe that was the politicians' way of thinking. Better to be talked about in a negative way than not to be talked about at all. What warped minds they had.

He heard the warble of a wren and marveled at the beautiful music a little speck of matter like a wren could make. He was proud of the fact that he liked almost all types of music, from rock and roll to The Buffalo Philharmonic, from the Beetles to Beethoven, but still he had to admit that nothing could compare favorably to that of Mother Nature's winged musicians. The wren's mate answered and soon there was a symphony of melodic trills filling the air.

"Music to my ears," he told them with a smile. He was in his glory.

The park was a favorite of local dog walkers but none came at the crack of dawn. This was *his* time, a time to commune with nature with no distractions. That's why, even though faint, the girl's voice seemed to attack him.

"Sophie, come here." She was obviously calling her dog...at the crack of dawn? She was close enough now that he could hear the sound of her footfalls as they crunched upon the dried pine needles. "Stay by me, punk'n. Don't want to lose you."

The Secret Monster Within

He hid behind some brush. He didn't have to strain to hear her anymore. She was coming closer with every step. No need to alert her to his presence. At least, not yet.

"What's the matter, Sophie? Why are you growling?"

He could never understand people who talked to their pets as though they could understand them, as though they would answer. *Why are you growling, Sophie?* He knew why. Sophie could sense his presence, and his mistress couldn't.

Sophie's growls turned to sharp yaps that were directed at him.

He peeked through the dense foliage and caught a glimpse of the noisy cur. It was one of those little yappy breeds, all hair and no substance. The girl had stopped walking and was searching the area. He could see her clearly now, and he saw the fear in her eyes.

She was pretty, just like the rest of them. And her dark brown hair fell in natural waves over her shoulders.

"Come here, sweetie." He was mimicking her call to her dog, but he whispered it to her instead.

"Sophie. Let's get out of here." The pretty girl surveyed the area around her. The look of fear had turned to panic.

And then she was there, right there in front of him. It was almost too easy. He reached out and his hands clasped her long slender throat.

And the dog's yapping must be stopped.

Chapter 7

Ken Lopez wasn't ashamed of it, in fact, he was rather proud of it if the truth were known, *it* being the fact that he had never gone to college. He had graduated from high school with honors, although the subject and the chance to brag of that little known fact seldom came up. But what did it matter? Look where he had gotten on sheer determination, and, yes, good luck.

His house was gigantic, though it seemed a bit hollow and empty now. He smiled as he remembered when it had housed both him and his wife and their three children. There was no denying how much he missed his sons and daughter now that they were grown and off on their own.

"So what!" he would grant those who brought it up, "I know the house is too big for just the two of us, but I just

The Secret Monster Within

can't give it up." It contained too many happy memories that had been a part of him and his family for too many years.

He swiveled his rocker so he might see the whole of his family room. It was monstrous, twenty by twenty-five feet, and it sported a brick fireplace that went from the floor to the two-story high cathedral ceiling. And this was just one of the many rooms that caused him to puff with pride. The upstairs' master bedroom was almost as large, not even counting the attached glamour bath and two walk-in closets. Two other full baths and three good-sized bedrooms, empty of inhabitants now, finished off the upper level.

The living room was small for easy conversation, but the library/den was huge. This was Ken's room, a place to work and a place to relax. The lower walls were two-thirds paneled in a deep mahogany, and he and Maureen had chosen to offset the rich wood base with a burgundy, gold and olive-green wallpaper. All of Ken's paper work and computer were hidden behind a beautifully carved wooden cupboard of matching wood that rested on his massive desk.

But Ken did not believe in all work and no play. Along with all these requisites needed for business, there was also a giant wall-mounted TV and the latest in stereo equipment. A leather couch and two recliners were each complemented by a wood and marble table topped with Tiffany lamps and Waterford crystal. But the best, as far as Ken was concerned, was the wall of books that surrounded the woodburning fireplace. This was *his* room, and he loved the look and feel of it.

They lived in what had popularly become known as a McMansion in an elite community in an elite town. Call it anything you like, but he was rightfully proud of what he had accomplished when you considered how much he had against him from the start.

His mother and baby sister had died when he was still a little boy, and that left him with a father who was a lost soul. Although his father continued to keep a roof over their heads and provided food and clothing, that was about it. There was little chance his father would or could be reported for cruelty because being cruel would require that he acknowledge he had a son.

The girl he had hired to look after Ken did an efficient job of it, but there was no love lost between the little boy and his hired caretaker. For her, it was just a job. And on the weekends when his dad was home, the days Ken so looked forward to, his father pretty much left him alone.

At first, Ken had been equally lost, but eventually he had toughened up and learned how to get what he wanted. This was to serve him well as an adult. OK, he granted, this tough-guy persona resulted in his not having too many friends, but so what. That was the price one had to pay, or at least that's what he kept telling himself.

After graduating from high school, he had scorned college and instead obtained employment at General Motors, one of western New York's largest employers. The money in the pocket was too much to turn down, and this is where he was working when he met Maureen O'Malley, the new receptionist.

Meeting Maureen had been gloriously wonderful. As the old song goes, she was *lovely to look at and delightful to know,* and best yet, she liked him. In fact, she liked him a lot, and the feeling was most assuredly mutual. Even his father had brightened after meeting her, and for the first time since his mother's death, his father began to show an interest in Ken and his future. Maureen was the light at the end of the tunnel, she was his salvation, his ticket to a happy life, and they were married shortly thereafter.

He had a good steady job with GM and was able to

The Secret Monster Within

provide for his family quite nicely. What else did he need? Nothing except an impossible dream. One day, while reading the want ads in the paper, he confided in his wife that he had always wanted to own a business of his own but knew that wish would always remain just that. He saw the empathy on his wife's face, and quickly assured her that his job with GM was just fine. "Honest," he said, "it's just one of those dreams we all have sometime in our lives," and he laughed it off.

But he obviously didn't know his wife as well as he thought he did. Unbeknownst to him, she had gone to his father and revealed his secret.

"You must be a sorcerer!" he later told her. "Dad has offered to loan me money to start a new business!" His father, this distant man who barely acknowledged his son's existence, was there for him now.

But soon after it was a fait accompli, Maureen wasn't sure if she had done the right thing. After all, Ken had been earning a great wage with terrific benefits, and they had already started a family. To top it off, they had just bought and moved into a house across the street from his father's house. Should they throw all this away on a chance? Both acknowledged that few new businesses actually succeed, and they knew that taking this chance was a crazy thing to do. But she had seen the look in Ken's eyes when he told her of his dream, so how could she deny him his chance?

Her heart was in her throat when Ken quit his job and bought an auto window glass tinting business. What have I done, she wondered? And the first year hadn't been easy. But under his wise supervision, the business had survived its first and second year, and then to everyone's surprise, it had succeeded beyond everyone's dreams during the third. Eventually, they left the West Side of Buffalo and moved to Amherst, and his father was repaid in full, both with money owed and with gratitude given.

Ken was remembering it all now, his trip from factory worker to successful business owner, as he surveyed his large house filled with expensive furnishings. He smiled as he thought of the two expensive cars sitting in their three-car garage, and pictured the yacht he had moored at Rich's Marina. He wished his mother had lived to see what a success her little boy had become.

***

Ken once again handed the paper to his wife. "Good God. There's been another one! And in Amherst again."

"What?" Maureen took the paper from her husband. "It hasn't been that long since he killed the Donovan girl. Seven years, nothing, and now," Maureen's body shook with revulsion, "two of them, just one month apart."

"It must be close to that. I'm not sure." Ken frowned in an obvious effort to remember. "But don't forget, Maureen, all the others happened in Buffalo." He emphasized the location. "These latest are happening within a three-mile radius of our house! Good Lord, watch yourself. Please."

Again Maureen reminded her husband of her blonde hair and her advanced age. "I'm safe, honey"

"I don't care what you say. This guy may change his MO, as you so aptly put it, just like that." He snapped his fingers to emphasize the short span of time he was trying to convey to her.

"You don't have to worry about me, Ken, but I am worried that this has happened just as Kyle and Rachel are coming here to visit." Her creased brow accentuated her concern.

Ken smiled at the thought of his daughter's visit. There were no words to describe how much he missed Kyle and

The Secret Monster Within

Rachel and even his bit off-the-wall son-in-law since they moved to California. It was too bad Terry couldn't come this time, but at least he would see his daughter and granddaughter. He was deliriously happy over the prospect of their visit.

The fact that the Lopez's two sons lived near them was a plus and certainly helped, but it still didn't make up for the empty space that his daughter's moving to the West Coast had left.

"I wish Terry could have come," Maureen said, "but he knew when he took that new job there would be no vacation this year. Thank goodness he's agreeable to letting Kyle and our granddaughter come anyway. We owe him for that." Maureen emphasized the latter.

"And we'll never let either of the girls go out alone," Ken promised.

***

Jen leaned over and said, "That's good, honey." Jen rubbed Katie Smith's shoulders and looked up from the picture the five-year-old had just finished coloring. The persistent knocking on the locked front door alerted her to the fact that someone wanted in. "I'll be right back," she told her charge.

She peered through the glass windows strategically placed in the door and was rewarded with the smiling face of her good friend, Ken Lopez.

"Hi, Mr. Lopez." She greeted him as she unlocked the door.

"Hi, Jen." Ken Lopez's continued smile was radiant.

"Oh," she said, as the meaning for his visit became clear, "I'll bet Kyle and Rachel are coming to visit you."

"Well then, I guess you know why I'm here." Ken

grinned at the perceptiveness of this young lady. She reminded him of his own absent daughter and this had resulted in his feeling a special kinship with her

"Mrs. Lopez and I missed you at church last week so we didn't get to tell you that we'd like to reserve a spot for Rachel at Playground For Kids." Ken made a sad face. "They'll only be here for a week."

"A week? Well, that should make for a nice visit. I know how much you miss Kyle and Rachel, and I'm sure you wish it could be longer, but," Jen's commiserate sad face brightened, "having them here for even a week should be a nice treat for you and Mrs. Lopez." It was no secret to the Wilkins how much the Lopez's missed their daughter. In fact, Ken never failed to mention it every time they met, either at church or socially.

Now he followed her lead and smiled back. "You know," he acknowledged, "even when they lived here, Kyle and her husband, Terry Border, lived a good distance from our house. We didn't see them that often. Maybe," he shrugged, "once a week at the most."

"It was because of this distance between us that Kyle was only too happy to use the baby-sitting service provided by Mrs. Longfellow's new business. Kyle went back to work as a nurse just as soon as Rachel reached Playground's required age of six months," he added as a means of explanation.

"Actually, I was the one that read about this service in the local paper, and I suggested to Kyle that she check it out. So as it was, Rachel was Playground's first enrollment. But I see business is booming since then." Ken raised his eyebrows and smiled as he spread his arm in a semi-circle to include all in the busy room.

"It was because Kyle proved to be such a loyal partaker of the new business that she has received special favors

The Secret Monster Within

from Mrs. Longfellow," Ken explained, "and that has held true through all these years, even after they moved away. "Mrs. Longfellow has promised she will always make room for Rachel whenever Kyle and my granddaughter come home to visit us."

"Oh, yes, I'm well aware of that, Mr. Lopez," Jen assured him. "Mrs. Longfellow isn't here today and I normally wouldn't feel free to grant a request like this, but I know she'll make room for Rachel, just like she always does. Rachel's very special to us, you know. She's such a cutie-pie."

"Why, thank you, Jen." Ken's smile lit up the room. "We think so."

"What date should I put down? I'll give the message to Mrs. Longfellow." Jen reached for a memo pad. "She'll be back tomorrow."

Ken pointed to the Saturday on the calendar that he expected Kyle and Rachel to arrive at their home. "We'll bring Rachel in the following Monday if that's OK with Mrs. Longfellow."

"I'm sure that will be all right. If not, I'll give you a call. We have your number, don't we?"

"Oh, yes. Been doing this for many years now."

"That's right. We'll look forward to seeing your little granddaughter again."

"Why thank you, Jen."

"You're welcome." Jen returned his warm smile since things seemed to be settled, but Mr. Lopez didn't seem ready to leave. Jen searched for something to say to fill the uncomfortable pause.

"Wasn't that awful about the latest victim of that monster? He killed her and her dog. Ugh." Jen closed her eyes in a futile effort to rid her mind of the picture. "I just can't figure this guy out. There was a rash of them so many years ago, then a seven-year respite. We thought we were done with him, but now," Jennifer shook her head in disbelief, "it looks like he's back, and he's murdered two in a row."

"I know, honey, and I don't know if I should say this..." Ken paused, and Jen could see he was debating whether to continue. She heard him draw a deep breath before he said, resolutely, "You know you are pretty, you're young and you have dark hair. Good God, girl, watch yourself, will you? You're his MO."

Ken shook his head and flicked his wrist in a dismissive way. "I'm sorry. That's my wife talking. I don't know beans about MOs or any of those other police abbreviations. All I know is you've got to be careful." He reached over to touch her arm. " You will watch it, won't you?"

"Thanks, Mr. Lopez. You can bet on it. I've taken Karate and self-defense courses. I'm ready for it if and when I need to be.

Chapter 8

Dan Halloway stared at the TV without seeing it. Trigger, his golden retriever, rested his head on his master's knee and Dan absent-mindedly scratched the dog's ear. It had been a full day, with another murder and no clues. Exhaustion was etched on his face, exhaustion and the blank look of a lonely man. He had no one with whom to share his thoughts or feelings. Being a bachelor was a lonely life.

He had tried marriage once, but being a cop and then a detective, had put the kebash on that once idyllic union. All the petty quarrels about the late nights, the never knowing when he would be home, the not being able to make plans with friends or family, and on and on, had taken their toll. It had gotten so bad, he was glad when it was over. But now, in retrospect, he could see where the fault lay, and it was with him. And look where he was now, a lonely man in a lonely apartment with only a dog to keep him company.

"Well, I've still got my job, Trigger." His laugh was bitter.

Dan had spent a lifetime being the idol of women. They swarmed about him like bees to a honey hive. He had his pick, and he had picked many. Tall, short, plump, skinny, blonde, brunette, or redhead, it didn't matter. They were conquests, and he was the master conquistador. It was a power feeder, and he, like many, enjoyed the feeling of power. But none left him fulfilled. None, until Brenda arrived quite by accident and that was a play on words that he often used to his own continual amusement.

He had dropped off one of his latest conquests, a girl whose name escaped him now, and was on his way home. It might have been the drinks, or the music, or just plain daydreaming, but he had run a stop sign and clipped the rear end of a minivan. It did damage to both cars, but it was worth it. That's how he and Brenda Lee Marcela had met.

As she emerged from the damaged van, Dan wanted to pinch himself in an effort to prove he was really there and that she was real. No, she couldn't be. This had to be a dream, and he literally shook his head in an effort to prove to himself that it wasn't. Certainly no mere mortal could be this beautiful.

She was tall and willowy, and she had a peaches and cream complexion that was flawless. Her honey-colored hair reached her shoulders and reflected the glow from the streetlight with a million little rays of light. Her eyes were crystal blue and were framed by a double layer of light brown lashes, attesting to the reality of her blonde hair. She had a full bust, a narrow waist, softly rounded hips, and

The Secret Monster Within

legs that seemed to go on forever. She was a dream come true, but she was real, one hundred percent real.

She had started off all fire and brimstone, a woman full of wrath for the damage done to her car, but he had tamed her as only he could. Before long, she was a pussycat and, of course, he had her address and phone number, as she did his.

That was the beginning of a true courtship and that was something he had never experienced before. He remembered the day he drove her to Cleveland to meet his parents and hoped it would go well. And it had. They were enthralled to meet this beauteous woman who was so warm and loving.

He could only hope it would go as well when he met her family. And it had. They liked him. They really liked him, and the feeling was mutual.

A date was set, and the months of preparation culminated in a lovely wedding. They spent their honeymoon on the beaches of Jamaica, where she proved to be as passionate in the art of love as she was fire and brimstone when she was angry.

The trouble started soon after they returned home. His job as a police officer demanded he be on call at all times, and the phone had no conscience when it came to time. It rang all hours of the night. There was really no use in making plans because the plans were often aborted at the last minute.

There were, however, still moments of love and passion. They were young, and in spite of the outside pressures, still in love. Brenda became pregnant a few months after their wedding, and a son was born nine months later.

Drew was Dan's pride and joy. He was a healthy baby who had inherited both his mother and father's blonde good looks. In fact, everyone told them their baby should be a model because he was so exceptionally beautiful. Of course there would be no such thing but, nevertheless, he puffed with pride.

Ten years passed, and the spats turned into downright fights. It became so unbearable, he dreaded going home. He would, in fact, often spend the night on the lumpy couch in his office.

They tried counseling but even that didn't work. The once idyllic marriage ended in a divorce, albeit a friendly one. So friendly, in fact, they would kid each other that if they had expended as much effort being as nice to each other during their marriage as they did during its break-up, maybe it would have worked. But then they would give a bitter laugh because both knew in their hearts that even that wouldn't have helped.

Dan moved to a comfortable apartment, while his wife and son remained in the large colonial home they had bought a few years earlier. He visited often and was as close to his son as any divorced father could be.

He became accustomed to his single life and worked his way up the ranks until he made detective. It was getting easier until the day he learned his wife, or make that exwife, was getting married again. He felt violated. Someone was stealing, touching his property, and there was nothing he could do about it.

He had met Brenda's fiancé, and in spite of himself, had immediately liked him. And George Preston was good with Drew, which was the most important trait his son's soon-to-be stepfather must possess.

He commended himself for how well he was handling it until the day of Brenda's wedding. He had been invited, but refused to go. As it turned out, it proved to be the toughest day of his life, and he could barely wait for it to be over.

That had been over ten years ago. Ten years plus of bachelor living, and he was bored and tired of being alone.

"Sorry, Trigger. Didn't mean to hurt your feelings."

Chapter 9

Her mother and father and all of her relatives still called her Barbie, but she was now a very mature twelve years of age and she insisted that all her friends call her Barbara. She would reluctantly accept Barb if need be, but no more Barbie, please.

She looked into the mirror for at least the fourth time that morning and smiled at her reflection. "No one would ever guess I was twelve," she cooed in a sultry voice to her reflection. She had matured early and there was no padding needed to fill out her size B cup. She pushed her shoulders back so she might admire the bust line all the better.

"Barbie," her mother called up the stairs. "Would you do me a favor? I need some eggs and I'm half-way through making this cake." Barb could hear the frustration in her mother's voice.

"OK, Mom. Just a sec," Barb shouted back.

Barbara checked her makeup, applied more lip-gloss, and combed her ebony-black hair before she came down the stairs to do her mother's bidding.

Carol Fairchild smiled at her daughter. "Thanks, honey. I could have sworn I had enough eggs but I forgot we used some this past Sunday." Carol handed her daughter a few dollars. "Get the large size. OK? I still have so much to do here."

"OK, Mom. Be right back."

"Hey, young lady," Carol shouted after her quickly departing daughter, "don't take any shortcuts. No walking through the woods," she said with great emphasis. "Promise."

Barbara raised her hand in a show of a solemn oath on her way out the door. "I promise." She had to fight to keep the smile from showing. Her mother didn't know it, but she always took the shortcut through the woods, and this day would be no different. Her mother took her mothering chores much too seriously.

"Where is that girl? It shouldn't be taking her this long to go to Greg's Grocery. I should have gone myself." Carol grimaced and raised her brown eyes in frustration. Her face was red from the heat of the oven that she hadn't bothered to turn off, and beads of sweat began to form under the straight dark bangs that almost touched her eyes. "I'll never get this cake baked in time."

Another look at the clock proved her daughter had been gone for almost an hour. "Even if she had done as she was told, and she better have, she should have been home some time ago. Company is coming for dinner tonight. She knows that, and the cake has to be baked and cooled by

The Secret Monster Within

then. What in the world is keeping her?" she spluttered with impatience.

Her husband, Norman Fairchild, wobbled his head back and forth. He had just arrived home and was being greeted with this tale of woe. He was a nice looking man with sandy hair, blue eyes and a thin-lipped mouth. He was quiet and soft-spoken and almost always maintained his cool. It took a lot to rile him, but Carol was getting on his nerves.

"Here," he said as he grabbed his car keys. The exasperation was clear. "I'll go looking for her. Don't want mommy to get all upset with company coming tonight."

"You don't have to get sarcastic about it," she snapped.

Carol took a deep breath and tried to compose herself. "I'm sorry, Norm, but she's taking so long. Actually, I'm concerned, and I really would feel better if you would go look for her."

Norm's face softened. "Sure, hon. I didn't mean to sound nasty, but you do get yourself into a ball of worry whenever we have company." He kissed his wife's cheek. "I'm sure Barbie is fine, but I'll get her to hightail it home when I find her. And the Morris's are good friends of ours, so relax."

"I know. I know." Carol shook her head at the hopelessness of it. "If I could only change the way I get when we're having company, but I can't. It's just me being me." Her shoulders sagged in a display of defeat. "Sorry."

Norm smiled. "Be right back," he assured her.

The clerk at Greg's told Norman Fairchild that his daughter had indeed been there, but that was some time ago. She had bought a dozen eggs and left in a hurry because her mother needed them to finish a cake she was making for company dinner tonight. He couldn't imagine why she hadn't arrived home.

Norm traversed the streets with his car once more and found no sign of his daughter. He couldn't believe that Barbie would do anything as foolish as walking through the woods since she had been told time and time again not to do so. But, he reminded himself, she was twelve years old, and twelve-year-olds don't always do what they are told.

Oh, please, please, don't have gone into the woods, he silently prayed, and please, please be OK. He parked the car and walked into the woods to look for his daughter.

She wasn't to be found, but he did find the carton of eggs lying under a maple tree. The carton and all twelve eggs were crushed.

***

"A twelve-year-old? Surely it's not The Monster." Dan looked at Bernie with skepticism.

"Well, at first glance, I'd agree. I can't believe he would go after someone so young, but," Bernie held the photo up to face level, "this twelve-year-old looks a lot older." They both stared at the photograph the Fairchilds had given them. "He could have been fooled."

"Well, there's no body, so this is nothing like the other ones. I think we've got a new freak to worry about. All I know is we've got to find her. The whole town's in an uproar." Dan stated the obvious.

"I know," Bernie acknowledged. "But where do we begin? The police have examined every bit of the woods where the eggs were found. We've sent the egg carton, as slimy as it was, to forensics. Nothing there." He shook his head at the futility of it all.

"There were footprints, albeit negligible ones, under the maple tree. They're working on that." Dan was grasping at straws.

The Secret Monster Within

***

The news was full of this latest horrific event, and the Amherst Town Council meeting was jam-packed with residents insisting on closure.

"The police are on this and doing everything they can." Supervisor Kmeche tried to calm the crowded room.

"Well, not enough!" A resident stood with a fisted arm stretched to the ceiling.

"He's right" Another resident stood in an effort to be heard.

"What do you suggest we do?" Supervisor Kmeche stared at the assemblage. His baldpate and big belly gave him a baby-like look that seemed to match his demeanor. He was obviously at a loss as to what to do.

The image of Barbara's mother as she appeared on TV was on everyone's mind. She had looked so young herself as she pleaded with the viewing audience to help her find her little girl. She was sobbing and the copious tears would melt the heart of anyone watching excepting, of course, the one who had abducted her daughter.

Ken Lopez was a good citizen. He had even contemplated running for councilman once, but had quickly discarded it when he saw the time it would take away from his business. Nevertheless, he attended every board meeting and was up-to-date on all subjects. Now he surveyed the room and saw the exasperation on everyone's face. He didn't know where the idea came from, but suddenly it was there. Ken rose to be heard.

"I have an idea," he shouted. The din slowly faded and the room was eventually quiet. "Why don't we all go through the woods together as a hunting party?" He looked about the room seeking support for this innovative idea. He was fairly tall with a Latin complexion, and his brown eyes glittered with enthusiasm as he realized he was the only one in the room who had offered to take charge.

And he wasn't to be disappointed. Everyone shouted his or her approval at once. The fact that the police force had already done so seemed to elude them at this moment.

***

Up till now, the area had been taped off as a possible crime scene and, as a result, no one had been allowed in the woods. It had been over a week since Barbara had disappeared, but now the wooded area was about to be opened to the public. The organized hunt was on for Sunday, and the media had offered to advertise for volunteers.

At first Police Chief Bernie Roper scoffed at the idea. Why use a group of untrained citizens to scan an area that the expert police force had already done? But he was at his wit's end as there were no clues, and if it was The Monster who had abducted Barbara, this scumbag was literally getting away with murder…again. The public was becoming more and more restless and frightened by the day. Who knows? Maybe someone would find that one elusive clue that would help solve this mystery, and if not, at least the public would feel they had been a part of seeking a solution. He hoped that might help calm the restive citizenship. Besides, at this unproductive point, he wasn't about to turn down any offer of help.

***

"What a heart you Amherst residents have," Bernie announced. "Look at this crowd." He was amazed at the vast number of people who had responded. There were well over two hundred unified citizens wanting to do whatever

The Secret Monster Within

they could to solve this terrible mystery.

Why had Barbara Fairchild disappeared, and where did she go? As much as everyone wanted to know the answer, each was afraid of what it might be. They knew this little girl had been asked to go to the grocery store to get eggs and had, in fact, done so. They also knew from all the information presented by her family that she was not the type to disappear on her own. The conclusion was obvious, but no one wanted to acknowledge it.

The police, including Chief Bernie Roper and his friend, Detective Dan Halloway, were at the park in an effort to organize the mass of volunteers. It wasn't easy, but they had managed to gather the group into one long line, an arm's length away from each other.

"Count off by tens," Dan shouted over the loudspeaker. "Every tenth person is your group's leader." Helen and John Colbert started the count, "One, two," with Nancy and Christopher Cranston following. Vanessa said a barely audible "five" with Troy shouting a booming "six". Jen and Vince voiced a clear "seven and eight". Maureen and Ken Lopez finished up the first group, with Maureen quickly changing places with her husband. "I don't want to be leader," she exclaimed with a wide-eyed grimace. Ken smiled and was only too happy to make the switch, and since Ken was the last of the group, he shouted a resounding "ten".

"OK. Let's go," he said as the leader, and each person in his group dropped his or her arm and moved forward as one.

The woods were thick and filled with heavy ground cover and brush. It wouldn't be an easy walk, but luckily it was flat, as was most of Buffalo, so there would be no strenuous hills to climb.

No one loved nature more than Jen, and normally she

would have been thrilled to walk through the woods. It had been so long since she had been able to do so, thanks to The Monster, but today brought no joy. She knew the chattering of a blue jay or the hoot of an owl mustn't distract her, and if she were lucky enough to see any creature of the woods, she must pay no attention. Her job was to search the area that had been assigned to her for clues of the missing child. This was very serious business and for once, Jen was taking it very seriously.

Everyone had been provided with plastic gloves, and they were advised to put anything they found in a plastic bag that had also been given to them by the police department. Normally there would have been a plethora of items, but the police had already combed the area. They had packed away pieces of material, buttons, cigarette stubs, condoms, both used and new, jewelry, pencils, pens, candy wrappers, and pieces of paper that were now in forensics for further scrutiny.

The volunteers were forced to admit that there was probably not much chance of their finding anything new but at least they felt better for having tried.

Chapter 10

The last seven and a half years that Vince Marotti had spent in Buffalo had tempered his accent a bit, but still no one had to guess where he was from. The *cahs* and the *pahks* said it all. No matter how much Jennifer tried, she couldn't get him to say "car" or "park". "Don't you know what an *r* sounds like?" she asked him. "Does the Boston alphabet go q *h* s t?"

Of course he had the perfect comeback. "Look who's talking. Your flat a's shatter my nerves. *I caan't do that. I caan do this.*" He jut his jaw out and spread his mouth wide, accentuating the flat "a" even more than any native of Buffalo would do. "Don't talk to me about accents," he told her. Then they both laughed.

Like most teenagers, Vince had no idea what he wanted

to be when he graduated from high school. He had done well in Business Law, so he opted to believe that his destiny was in the legal field. Harvard was right at his doorstep, but neither his grades nor his parents' bank account would enable him to consider that as a venue. However, the University at Buffalo was highly praised for its law school and, although not inexpensive, it was still within the Marotti family's financial sphere as long as he was willing to work part-time to help out. And so, Buffalo it was.

He found a two-room apartment that was extremely reasonable, at least compared to Boston's real estate prices, and he couldn't believe his luck. The large kitchen was lined with white painted wood cupboards, some of which had frosted glass installed in the front panel. The landlord informed him this was all the rage in the '30's, 1930's that was. He understood that this very same style was coming into vogue again.

Vince wasn't sure if he liked the fact that the kitchen was furnished with an antique gas stove that stood on four high legs, and a refrigerator that was so old, it needed defrosting.

"They don't make 'em like that anymore," his prospective landlord had advised him. Vince wisely chose not to reply.

His bathroom was old-fashioned as well, with a pedestal sink—yes, he had been told, that's the way they made them close to a century ago—and a free standing clawfooted bathtub. A shower faucet had been added to the front of it, and the 1930's black and white hexagon tile floor was protected from the spray by an inexpensive striped plastic shower curtain that surrounded the tub.

The combination living room/bedroom was large, but empty. Vince would have to furnish it, but that was a minor problem, so he readily agreed to the low rental price.

The Secret Monster Within

A college buddy of his had advised him where to shop. So the gray futon didn't match the brown rug. Who cared? He didn't.

"So what?" Vince had informed his style-conscious mother. "It works as a sofa and a bed. It's fine, Mom." His mother would later give him a few taupe pillows to throw on the futon to soften the look.

He had found the combination bed/couch at the Salvation Army Store for only thirty dollars, and for five bucks more, they had thrown in a chipped coffee table. In addition, he had found a wooden rocker and an upholstered recliner, which was brown. Vince made sure his mother noticed that the recliner did match the rug.

The TV his parents had given him was one they no longer used, but it worked. He had placed it on an old entertainment center he had purchased at The Goodwill for easy viewing.

His parents had been only too happy to give him his old desk, and that's where he kept his computer, stereo, I-Pod, and cell phone. What else did he need? Vince had come from an upper middle class family, but he was very easy to please when it came to physical comforts.

It was a different story, however, when it came to his curriculum. It took him almost two years to realize that the field of law was not where he belonged. He hated it. But he continued his love of crunching numbers, so the following year he started from scratch and majored in accounting.

His part-time job as a collection agent grew. He was doing so well at it, in fact, that he found himself putting more hours into it then he should. This resulted in his spending less time on his studies, and so here he was, over seven years later, still working on his four-year degree.

Actually, he didn't mind one bit. Being a long-time student had begun to grow on him. Besides, he loved Buffalo and he liked his job. But best of all, he had met Jennifer Wilkins.

He would never forget that night. He and his buddies had gone to a local bar, the same one they went to every Saturday night. It was fun, but again, the same old, same old. That is, until she walked in. He had turned around on the swivel barstool with beer in hand just as the door opened, and *she* came in. He could hardly catch his breath.

She was so tiny, so cute, so absolutely, wonderfully perfect in every way. He loved the way her short curly hair formed a dark cap that accentuated her creamy white face. And now he knew what the poets meant when they compared some blue eyes to sapphires. Never could a jewel win in such a competition. And, tiny as she was, her figure was perfect. God, look at those full round breasts, tiny waist and barely there hips. And even though short, her legs were perfectly formed. He was running through the full litany, and could find no fault whatsoever. She was a dream come true.

Don't foul this up, he kept telling himself. God, please don't foul this up.

He caught her eye, and she returned his smile.

Thank you, God. Thank you. It was a good beginning. Now if he just didn't mess it up by saying something stupid. She came to the bar with her group of friends and ordered a beer, and there she was, right behind him.

"Hi," he said.

"Hi." She was still smiling.

The place was full and there were no seats available. "Here," he said. "Want my seat?"

She had thanked him but said she was with friends, this very same group of friends who had witnessed the electricity that emanated between the two of them.

"Hey, grab a seat, Jen," one of them said. "We'll see you later."

The Secret Monster Within

But they hadn't. Jen and Vince were a twosome from that moment on.

She was the lynch pin, the real reason why he couldn't leave to go back to Boston. He was head over heels in love, and wonder of wonders, it seemed it was reciprocal.

"What a lucky day it was when I met you," he whispered in her ear once more.

***

Most of the nation accepted the fourth of July as Independence Day, but to Jen, it would always be June 20. Her parents called it moving day, but nevertheless, here she was, at last living on her own and proud of it.

OK, she had to admit she missed coming home to a hot supper, having her clothes washed and folded, having easy access to a car ride, be it her mother's or her father's. It was a lot to give up, but look at me, she said to herself. No one to answer to. I am finally an independent adult.

In the back of her mind, Jen knew she had to qualify that since Donna and Rob did seem to act as surrogate parents but, basically, she was on her own. She loved being able to say that. All that was lacking was a means of transportation.

How she rued the day she had let Jewel drive her car, the one her parents had given her as a graduation gift from high school. It wasn't new and it wasn't the make she would have picked, but it did manage to do all that it was intended to do. It was reliable and it got her to whatever her destination with no modicum of trouble. As it was, her destination was more often than not either college classes or the mall.

And then came that fateful night. Jewel Johnson, her best friend from forever ago, had begged and begged to let her drive till she could stand it no more.

Jen finally relented and said, "If I let you do it, you must be doubly careful, Jewel. It's raining, so drive slowly. Promise?" Jewel raised her hand and swore she would be as careful as anyone could be.

Jen knew it was wrong, but what the heck. Jewel was one of the brightest girls she knew, although she had to admit to herself, not one of the most sensible. Oh well, it was only a half-hour's drive. What could happen?

Nothing, actually. Nothing at all until Jewel almost missed the drive into the mall. "Oh, there it is," she exclaimed, while slamming on the brakes and turning the steering wheel as far to the left as possible. The combination of a slick road and the too-quick turn spun the car out of control. Both Jewel and Jen screamed as the car's front fender smashed into the guard post that sat sentinel at the entrance to the Galleria Mall. Jen would never forget the sound of the crushing metal or the noise of the air bags exploding.

Both girls stared at each other in a state of bewilderment. What had happened? It took a moment or two before each realized the consequences of their actions. "My God. I don't have a license." Jewel stated the obvious. "What will they do to me? Or to you?"

"Quick. Change seats, Jewel." Jen said this with no thought to the future. And so it was that Jen's record was blemished, her first car was totaled, and her insurance rates went off the roof.

And she had been car-less ever since.

Chapter 11

"There she is!" Maureen raised her arm and leapt into the air so her daughter might see her in the crowd that was awaiting friends and relatives just deplaning. Ken grinned and waved his arm too.

"Over here, honey," he shouted.

Kyle smiled broadly and waved back. Although she had inherited her mother's light complexion, everything else about her was a carbon of her father. No one would ever guess she was Maureen's daughter as well.

"Lucky for me I saw her when she was born, or I wouldn't have believed it either." Maureen would laugh as she explained this to all the friends and family members who felt it necessary to comment on their obvious differences. She would then remind everyone she had two blonde blue-eyed sons "So there." She would get the last word after all.

It had been months since Kyle had been home, and it felt so good to be here at last. There was a lot to be said about California, but it just wasn't home. Neither of her brothers was there to meet her as they both worked at their father's business on Saturdays, but she knew they and their families would be gathered around her parents' table at dinner tonight. Her stomach rumbled as she thought of the delicious home-cooked meal her mother would have prepared.

After hugs and kisses, Ken turned to his granddaughter. "Who is this beauty you brought with you? Is this my granddaughter?" He pretended to be unsure as he stared into the green eyes of the little girl who smiled back at him. He caressed her dark red hair and then bent to hug her, and was rewarded with one in return.

"Look at the dolly mommy and daddy gave me for the trip. Isn't she cute?" Rachel held out the baby doll for both grandparents to see.

"Oh, honey," Maureen bent to kiss her granddaughter, "she's almost as cute as you."

The evening was not a disappointment. It was so good to see her brothers and sister-in-laws once more, and, of course, their children! "What a prolific pair of guys you are." Kyle loved razzing them and they took it in good humor.

"Well, Sis, guess you've got a lot of catching up to do." Her brother, Larry, grinned and spread his hands to include his five and the four that belonged to their brother, Denny.

Kyle raised her hands in surrender. "No contest. You win." Kyle laughed and then asked them to pass the salsa sauce

The Secret Monster Within

The dining room of the Lopez's spacious house was huge, and seemed even larger since four round pillars separated it from the living room rather than the usual solid wall. The mahogany dining table seated the seventeen guests with no sense of crowding, although some of the smaller children had to be propped up with boosters. The large brass and crystal chandelier sparkled overhead, matching the four sconces on the wall.

Dinner was all she had hoped it would be. No one could beat Maureen when it came to the culinary arts. Although she was of Irish and German descent, she would never have to take a back seat to anyone when it came to cooking Spanish-style foods. She had studied and learned well through the years.

"Umm." Kyle closed her eyes in ecstasy as she savored the flavor of hard and soft tacos, enchiladas, and burritos. Even Rachel, who was normally a very fussy eater, was cleaning her plate.

"Look how well Rachel is eating." Maureen pointed to her granddaughter with pride. "You know, I was going to make a nice casserole, but I knew Rachel likes these types of food," Maureen said as she spread her hand to include all the bounty on the table, "so this dinner was made special for my very special granddaughter." Maureen kissed the air in the direction of the honored guest. "I hope you folks don't mind," she said as she glanced at the rest of her family.

"Mom, are you kidding? You should open a cooking school. You'd be a millionaire," Kyle said with no obvious recognition of the fact that her mother already was. She took another mouthful and closed her eyes once more as a show of appreciation.

"I've told her that many times." Ken laughed as he raised his glass of Sangria in a manner of tribute to his wife.

"Amen." All at the table raised their glasses in mutual agreement.

***

Rachel Lopez had attended Mrs. Longfellow's Playground For Kids from the time she was six months old. "How many years is that now, honey?" Mrs. Longfellow asked.

Rachel looked puzzled until Mrs. Longfellow asked how old she was.

"Oh." She brightened at having an answer. "I'm eight." She held up eight fingers so there would be no doubt.

"Well, then, I guess you've been coming here for eight years. I just opened for business the year you were born. You were my first customer, you know."

"Was I?" Rachel knew that somehow this made her special.

"Yes, you were, honey." Mrs. Longfellow bent to give Rachel a hug and a kiss. "And it's always so nice to see you. We've missed you since you moved away, and we're so happy when you can come visit us."

Rachel didn't know what to say, so she just smiled. She instinctively liked Mrs. Longfellow, and also Miss Wilkins, who had been a part of Playground For Kids these past two years.

"Hey," Jen said. "How about a hug and a kiss for me." Rachel shyly offered her cheek and allowed her being to be squeezed once more.

Chapter 12

The trees glowed pink in the rosy glow of dawn. No need to worry about anyone interrupting him this morning. Ever since he had killed Sally Swayzac and her yappy dog, no one dared come to the park this early. It was a relief in one way, but a disappointment in another. It had been an unexpected rush when he had encountered her that early summer morn. Now in the crisp coolness of autumn, it was eerily silent, with no promise of any such excitement.

He thought about her as he walked the perimeter of the lovely park. She had been one of the prettier victims and one of the most satisfying to watch as he saw the life leave her vibrant body. Most of his *Thrills* as he called them were planned, right down to the time and place. He knew who habitually walked and he knew where and when they walked. Their steady routines were the death of them. He couldn't resist a chuckle when a new thought occurred to him. They weren't steady routines; they were deadly ones. Yes, *deadly routines,* he mused. That was funny, wasn't it?

But his chances of additional thrills were becoming more and more remote. The news media were broadcasting warnings, and the viewing public was taking heed. Damn! He had to find a new prospect. The tension was building up inside of him and threatened to explode.

He heard a rustle in the brush. Could it be? Had someone dared to defy all the advertised warnings? Was he going to get lucky? He knelt behind a lilac bush that had just started losing its leaves, and this gave him the distinct advantage of being able to see through it quite nicely.

His heart began to pound at an uncommonly fast speed as the anticipation built up within him. Please, please, be a pretty brunette. Whoever it was, he or she was coming closer now. He prepared to leap, to clasp his hands around that delicate length of throat, and that's when he saw it...an ugly wild turkey.

The disappointment was overwhelming and it turned to anger at this intruder who didn't fulfill his fantasy. "Come here, you creature," he snarled at the gobbling bird. The turkey turned to run, but faced a thicket of brush that it couldn't penetrate. It was still searching for a means of escape when two hands grabbed its neck. All the anger and disappointment in the identity of his intended victim coursed through his veins and came out in his hands. He twisted the body one way and the head the other. He could hear the neck bones crack, and he felt some relief at last.

Not as satisfying as a petty brunette, but at least it was something.

Chapter 13

Vince stared into her eyes and smiled. "You have a young Elizabeth Taylor quality about you," he said.

"What? Are you kidding? She was gorgeous." Jen scoffed at the comparison.

"You are gorgeous. I've told you so a million times. Why won't you believe me? You've got the same flawless white skin as Elizabeth Taylor, the same violet eyes, those black arched eyebrows, the same cupie-bow lips, the same voluptuous body. I'm telling you, you look like Elizabeth Taylor when she was young." He said it with a vengeance and looked hurt that she wouldn't graciously accept these feelings that came straight from his heart.

"Oh, Vince. You're just too good to me." Jen reached

to put her arms around his neck and pulled him down to her level. "Give me a kiss, you Italian hunk."

Vince held her tightly and brushed his lips softly against hers. With closed eyes, he delighted in the sensation.

"I love you, Jennifer Wilkins, more than I can say," he whispered

"And I love you, Vince. Oh, God, I love you so much." Jen pressed her body against his and she felt the male hardness of him.

He kissed her brow, then her cheek, and now her lips once more. He so loved those beautiful lips that begged for passion and now his tongue forced her mouth to open.

Her breathing came in gasps as his hand softly caressed her breast. She was writhing with desire as he laid her upon his bed. Slowly, ever so slowly, his hand traveled the course from her breast to her stomach, touching her softly, closer and closer to the area where she was aflame. She was lost in a world of want and need, and only he could fulfill these desires.

As his hands found the prize, her moans turned to screams of delight and she arched her back, demanding to be taken.

Vince fumbled with his belt and zipper, and he quickly removed his trousers. She cried out with pleasure as he fulfilled her need.

Now she was lost in a swirling world of ecstasy, without a thought to the future. There was only one time and that time was now, this moment, this very moment of sheer delight. She felt his warm maleness flow into her, and she didn't care.

He shuddered and collapsed with his full weight pressed upon her tiny body and his heavy breathing roared in her ears. It took a minute before he came to his senses

The Secret Monster Within

and he realized how heavy his dead weight must be on her delicate frame. Now he rolled on his side, and his encircled arms carried her with him so she was but inches away from his face. He smiled at her and she smiled back.

"I love you," she whispered, as she kissed the sweat beads from his brow.

"That was wonderful, Jen. You're a sex machine." He brushed the damp hair back from her face.

"Only because I have a master lover." Jen wrinkled her nose and kissed his.

"I love you, with all my heart." He smiled and kissed her once more.

"When are we going to make it legal?" She knew the answer but she wanted to hear it once more.

"You know when." He laughed. "As soon as I get my degree and a decent job." He leaned up on his elbow and looked down at her. "You'd better get going with those wedding plans. That's not that much longer, you know."

How she loved to hear those words, *not much longer*. They were music to her ears. "I can hardly wait. Mrs. Jennifer Marotti," she said with eyes closed. " I like it."

"Not as much as I do."

***

There is an old vaudevillian joke that Buffalo has two seasons: winter and the fourth of July. That is a joke, of course, but anyone who has lived in Buffalo acknowledges that its winters are too cold, too snowy, and much too long. Of course, there are those winter sports enthusiasts who bravely defend the long Buffalo winters and are only too happy to list the plusses of ice fishing, skiing, ice skating, and sledding. But for the rest of the populous who are not of this ilk, each breathes a sigh of relief at the first signs of spring. Sadly though, even that season has been shortened enough that some years it appeared to be non-existent.

Oldsters would tell of a time when you could count on April to be a full-blown advertisement for a month of Spring, but lately it seems to have lost its flower power. Granted, it is still the month when you can count on seeing an early-returning robin and hear the trill of his beautiful song, or gasp with delight at the daffodils that bravely peek their colorful heads through a thin layer of snow, but that is all she will grant you. April storms of sleet and snow are not that unusual anymore.

It is now the month of May that has overtaken April in its viability to be called a true spring month, although even that is mercurial. Buffalonians joke that they can go to bed on an unbearably warm night in May with the air conditioning blasting, and wake up to a freak cold spell, or visa versa. And so what ensues is a wintry April, a volatile May, and then, suddenly, it's June, and just like that, summer is here. No, no one in Buffalo would brag about the season of winter and oftentimes, spring.

But the unadvertised seasons of summer and fall make up for it, with the month of October being a true work of art. Buffalo's wide arrays of trees change from their gossamer summer gowns of green to flamboyant shades of red and orange and yellow, with resulting landscapes that are breathtaking.

Donna had put on a light sweatshirt before carrying her palette of oil paints, an easel, and a stretched canvas to the back yard. The sky was a brilliant shade of blue with little puffs of marshmallow clouds playing tag. This was the backdrop upon which the flaming colors of the trees glowed in all their glory. Donna absorbed the loveliness of it all.

Yesterday she had used charcoal to sketch the place-

The Secret Monster Within

ment of the trees on her canvas, but today was the frosting on the cake, the day she would actually dab on the colorful oils with brush and palette knife, bringing the painting to life.

She was so absorbed in her work that she didn't hear the footsteps behind her.

"Do you mind if I watch?"

Donna almost jumped out of her skin as she turned and saw Jen.

"Oh, my gosh, Jen." She put her hand over her heart. "You gave me quite a scare."

"I'm sorry. I thought you heard me coming." Jennifer was full of apologies. "I'd love to watch though, if you don't mind."

"Of course. I'd be honored. Pull up a garden chair and sit beside me." Donna was all smiles now.

Jen was already impressed with the charcoal sketch. "I love what you've drawn," she told Donna.

"Thanks. This is just the skeleton, but now we dress it up." Donna laughed as she dipped her brush into the paint she had just mixed on her palette. "As you can see, I've already painted the top third of the canvas blue. I've sketched the trees on top of that. Always start from the back and work forward."

Jen loved art in any form, but had never taken any lessons. She was absorbing the bits and pieces that Donna was sharing with great relish.

"Now I'll add a few fluffs of clouds." Donna mixed white paint with a touch of blue. "Never paint anything pure white," she told Jen, "except for some striking accents. We'll add a little yellow to this too."

Jen was amazed as she watched Donna soft brush the edges of the off-white clouds so they appeared to be almost gauze-like, just like the ones in the sky above them.

"Wow."

"Thanks, Jen. One of my favorite critiques."

Donna continued with the painting, applying large globs of color with her palette knife. "First the trunk and the branches. We'll add the leaves later. Look how quickly it's done with a knife. It would take ages to do with a brush. And don't you just love the texture?"

"Oh, yes, I do. I can almost feel the bark." Jen was in awe as the sketch was being transformed into a beautiful painting.

Donna was enjoying the admiration she was receiving. "Here, Jen. Try it." Donna handed her the knife.

"What? Oh, never!" Jen recoiled from the offered knife. "I couldn't."

"You don't know until you try. It's easy. I promise. Here." Donna pressed the palette knife into Jen's tiny hand. "Don't be afraid. That's the beauty of oil paint. I can scrape off what I don't like and paint over it. No problemo."

Jen's hand was shaking as she laid a glob of green paint on the canvas.

"Pretend you're frosting a cake. Swirl it just a little, like this." Donna took another knife and showed Jen how to do it.

Jen did as she was told and paused to admire the leaf she had just created with one twist of her wrist. "Oh, my gosh. Look at that."

"Do another one," Donna said.

"Really? OK." Jen did another, and then another. This was so much fun.

"I'll tell you what," Donna said. "I have to finish this because I'm entering it in a contest. But," she paused to enrich the suspense, "if you want to buy a few supplies, I'll be happy to give you some lessons and then you can do some of your own. How would you like that?"

The Secret Monster Within

Jen knew she couldn't afford the lessons, but didn't want to spoil the moment. "Thanks, Donna. That would be wonderful."

***

He couldn't believe how much Jen looked like her, the one he had loved so much, then hated so much. She was the same size, tiny like a doll, and she had the same hair, almost blue-black, and it was curly just like hers. And she had the same full round breasts and narrow hips. She, above all others, should die, just like her.

But how could he? Jen? No, not Jen.

Jen had blue eyes. Hers had been brown. Was this what was keeping The Monster that lived within him from killing her? Other than the blue eyes, everything else was so much like her that it gave him chills. But those blue eyes. Maybe that would save her. Oh how he hoped so.

Please, please, please he begged the inner fiend in him. Don't kill Jen. Please don't kill Jen. He thought of how he would feel if and when he did, and it brought tears to his eyes. How incredibly awful it would be...

and how gloriously satisfying.

Chapter 14

The dorm room was small, but big enough for two single beds, two dressers, and all the latest electronic toys available to any seventeen-year-old. Tracy Goldsmith was texting messages while listening to her iPod. Her head and feet bobbed with the beat of the music and still she didn't miss a word in her message to Robin, her roommate.

where go tonight

Tracy punched the keys with alarming speed.

Robin wasn't quite as fast, but she didn't waste any words either.

evans. coming?

Late class meet Ev later.

K. syl

The Secret Monster Within

"Where is that girl?" Robin shouted above the ear-splitting music. Everyone shrugged his or her shoulders in a who-knows gesture. Robin's teenaged brow furrowed into worry lines. This was definitely not like Tracy.

This was Robin Windsong's first year of college, her first year of being on her own, and it had all been overwhelming. When she first arrived, there was so much to think about with regard to schedules and options, and there was so much to worry about, such as whom will I get as a roommate? The luck of the draw could make or break the next four years. What if it turned out to be someone she hated?

Her assigned room was empty, and she had just finished unpacking her suitcases and earmarking the bed by the window as hers when the door opened, and in walked this tiny brunette doll. "Hi," the talking doll said. "My name's Tracy Goldsmith. What's yours?" Her smile and offered hand had won Robin over immediately. They were fast friends from that day forward.

And now, where was she? Tracy was never late, and she never went back on her word unless something important came up, and then you could count on a phone call with detailed explanations. "She'd better have one hell of a good explanation for scaring me like this." Robin shouted her warning to the group sitting at her table.

It was Friday night and no one left till the last song was played, so it was three o'clock in the morning when the group piled into Dick's van. He dropped each off at their dorm before he headed for his. Robin was last, and she waved him a goodbye.

She noticed the broken light over the door and wondered who would have the nerve to do such an act of destruction. Some wise ass was her first thought. She shook her head at the juvenile behavior and unlocked the door to her dorm building.

It was the middle of the morning, and some of the students had returned from their evening sojourns by then, so she walked as quietly as possible. She knew some would already be asleep.

And at first, Robin didn't want to waken a sleeping Tracy either, but then her anger welled and she thought, why shouldn't I? She didn't show up and she never called. That was rude and thoughtless. Why should I care if I wake her up? "To hell with it," she scolded the closed door, and she opened it with as much noise as possible. There, that should do it. If that didn't wake her up, nothing would except, maybe, light. Robin switched the overhead light switch to the *On* position.

Robin stared at Tracy's bed and it looked no different than it had the morning before. It was roughly made and it was empty. Tracy hadn't shown up at The Evans, and she wasn't in her dorm. And it was three-thirty in the morning.

***

When Tracy left her class, it was after eight, and she did what she always did. The Evans had drinks and good music, but the food was not to her liking. Instead, she walked to The Diner, her favorite place to grab a bite. Saturday of last week was the day they had to turn the clocks back, and it was dark when she left the restaurant. How she hated that fallback day since it made the days so short. She missed those summer evenings that were sun-bright right up to nine o'clock. But, how are you going to fight nature or city hall?

She still had her books and notes from her last class and didn't want to be bothered with them at The Evans. It was

The Secret Monster Within

only a short distance to her dorm where she would drop them off, just as she always did, and then a quick bus ride from there to the Evans.

The campus seemed deserted but that was typical of a Friday night. Students spent all week barricaded in their rooms and Friday was Get-Free Night. If you were in, you were either dead or very sick. Obviously, no one was either.

There were plenty of lights, the college had seen to that, but for some reason, the light over the door to her dorm had been broken. As she fumbled for her key, she could see the silver shards lying on the ground.

Her head was bent. That really made it very inconvenient. He crept up behind her and cleared his throat. She looked up to see who was there, just as he knew she would. Now it was easy.

Chapter 15

"How does he get away with it?" Bernie smashed his fist on the tabletop in disgust.

"I don't know." Dan shook his head with a great show of weariness. "He doesn't leave a clue. We have no idea who or what we are looking for. All we know for sure is he's got to be mentally unbalanced."

"Well, what else do we know?" Bernie started writing on the blank wipe-off board in front of him. "Let's list whatever facts we have. Everybody here put on your thinking caps and shout out whatever you can remember." He turned to the group of police that had been called to this special meeting. Amherst citizens were on the verge of revolt.

"Let's start with seven years ago. There were twelve

The Secret Monster Within

murders, all in Buffalo. Twelve!" Bernie looked at the group of veteran police officers with a look that said it all. Twelve murders committed seven long years ago, and still no idea who the man might be that caused the deaths of these lovely young women.

There were two easels set alongside the wipe-off board. Bernie used his pointer to indicate the twelve victims from so long ago. "Look at them. What do you see?"

The rows of blue uniforms sat silently.

"Speak up!" Bernie smashed the pointer on the table.

Officer John Corey raised his hand and said, "I see twelve exceptionally pretty girls, all young, still in their twenties, and all brunettes."

"Oh," he added. "And all short."

"Good, John." Bernie wrote these observations on the board. No. 1. Pretty girls, 2. All in their twenties, 3. All brunettes, and 4. All short. "That's a start."

Officer Charlotte Miller raised her hand.

"Yes, Char. What have you got?" Bernie nodded his OK.

"They were all strangled, but there were no marks that would indicate it had been done with a rope or anything like a rope. He must have used his hands."

"Good." Bernie marked that down as No. 5.

Now everybody was shouting out thoughts at once.

"Whoa. One at a time." Bernie was pleased that his group of police officers was finally getting into this.

"There's no DNA so we know he uses gloves. Plastic ones."

"Right on, Cameron. Good one." Bernie wrote that down as No. 6.

"Most of them, though not all, were done on bike paths, or in wooded areas."

"That's No. 7," Bernie said as he wrote it on the board.

Paul McLaughlin raised his hand. "We've found through research," he said, "that all of these girls pretty much followed a routine. They used these same paths every day, either as a means of exercise or as a way to get to work or school. This monster must have checked their routines and learned when he would most likely encounter them in a remote area. That leaves us with a strong suspicion that he lived in Buffalo where all these murders occurred seven years ago."

Bernie wrote that down as No. 8. "A very important point, Paul. Good work."

"Now they're all happening in Amherst. Could he have moved here?"

"Another good point, Kevin. Number 9. More?" Bernie knew what was coming.

"But none of them were raped." Sgt. Bill Schanzer said what all of them were thinking.

"And didn't that surprise us all? Yep, no rapes. That's No. 10." Bernie added it to the list.

"And, of course," Bernie added, "there is his signature act that tells us they were all done by the same man." Bernie observed the nodding of heads. "We all know what that is, but we're keeping that a secret. If anyone of you lets it out, your job is history. Believe me when I tell you that!"

"And now that brings us to the present time." Bernie moved to the second easel upon which the pictures of the latest victims were posted.

"What do we see here?"

Officer Brandi Seigel shook her head and said, "Pretty much the same as seven years ago. Pretty young girls, all brunettes. Strangled in the same manner with no DNA. But what about this one?" Brandi pointed to the glamour picture of Barbara Fairchild.

"Well, as you know," Bernie said, "we haven't found

The Secret Monster Within

the body, so we can't be sure she is a victim of The Monster. We have her picture up here because it happened in the same time frame as the rest of them. We know The Monster preys on girls who are in their twenties, but even though Barbara is only twelve, don't tell me she doesn't look twenty-something."

"I'm afraid all that make-up, fancy hair do, and grown-up clothes was her death sentence." Dan said what everyone was thinking.

"Poor child." Bernie touched her picture, then turned away.

"Again," he continued, "the signature act on the rest of the girls is the same as The Monster of seven years ago, and since that's never been revealed, we know it's not a copy-cat. It's the same man, and when I say *man*, I use the term loosely. We all know what he is. Now if we only knew who he is."

"We need a break. That's for sure." Dan pretty much summed up everyone's opinion.

"OK, ladies and gentlemen. You know what we've got and you know what we need. Do your best and report anything that might be relevant to this case. Anything at all." Bernie dismissed the meeting with little to show for it.

Chapter 16

Jen had a history of late periods, so missing this one was no exception. And, even now, there would be no red flags except for the morning nausea. Please, please she prayed, don't let it be. There had been just that one time without protection. Only one time! It wouldn't be fair. But then, life's not always fair, is it?

Mrs. Longfellow took notice of Jen's morning nausea but chose not to comment on it. She would just wait and see, and hope her fears would not be realized.

Jennifer was at first torn whether to use the early pregnancy test or not, but it proved to be an easy choice since she was fearful of what the results might be. She was thinking and feeling afraid a lot lately. She opted, just like Mrs. Longfellow, to wait and see… and pray.

The Secret Monster Within

***

Donna knew what Jen earned at Playground For Kids. It was enough to pay the rent and buy a little food, but not much else. There wasn't even enough left over after major expenses to save for a car, something Jen desperately needed, so to ask her to pay for art lessons was a pie in the sky dream. Still, Donna had seen the glow, the eagerness to learn, that had shown through Jen's eyes while she watched her painting in the back yard.

"Jen. You have Saturdays and Sundays off, right?" Donna asked the question even though she knew the answer.

"Yes, that's right," Jen acknowledged.

"Well, since I love to paint, and you've shown an interest in learning, how would you like to join me on Saturday morning for a little one-on-one art instruction, around ten o'clock? You'll be up by then, won't you?"

Jen wanted to leap at the chance, but knew she couldn't afford it. "Oh, thanks, Donna. I'd love to, but I really don't have the money for lessons." Jen made a sad face, and then smiled. "Hey, thanks for asking though. I really would have loved doing that."

"I know what you make, Jen, and I know you can't afford art lessons. I'm offering these lessons gratis for two reasons: one because I love to paint, and two, because I saw how interested you were the other day. Any teacher would give anything to find a student who cares as much about the genre as you seemed to. One to two hours depending, ten AM, Saturday mornings, free of charge for one of my favorite people. How about it?"

Donna knew that Jen usually slept in late on Saturdays, but this was best for her schedule, so take it or leave it.

"Donna. Really?" Jen hugged her friend. "I don't know

how to thank you."

"You already have." Donna smiled and reminded her, "Next Saturday, ten o'clock. Up and at 'em, right?"

"You got it. And again, thanks so much."

Jen set the alarm. She knew if she didn't, she would sleep right through her allotted art lesson. Missing an hour or two of sleep wasn't a bad price to pay... not for free art classes.

But, of course, there was that morning nausea. It hadn't abated, and she was becoming more and more convinced that she was pregnant. What would she do if it turned out to be true?

Again, nothing to do but pray and wait, and pray again.

"All set?" Donna welcomed her with a smile and a glance at her watch that proved Jen was right on time. It was ten o'clock exactly.

"I sure am." Jen smiled back. She didn't think it prudent to disclose that she had gotten up very early in order to get through that morning nausea. She felt fine now.

"Well, sit here." Donna indicated the chair next to her. She was still using the back yard, but the days were getting colder. "We might have to use my inside studio starting next week. This crisp weather is invigorating, but there's a limit to what we can take." She laughed as she thought of Buffalo's notorious winters.

"Oh, I don't mind the cold. No one loves the outdoors more than I do, and it's beautiful today," Jen said as she scanned the blue sky.

"I thought we'd start with some basics." Donna reached for a stretched canvas.

"Lesson number one will be on canvases. You can buy stretched ones just like this" Donna said as she held up a finished product that she had bought at the art store. "Or, if

The Secret Monster Within

you want to save money, and I know you do, you can stretch your own."

"Really?"

"Yes. It's very simple. Here, watch me." Donna grabbed a wooden frame that measured 8 x 11 inches. "You can even buy separate pieces of wood frames in different measurements to make your own frame that will cost less then a ready-made one, but I thought we'd start with this one for today."

"As you can see, I've bought a roll of canvas which I can cut to any size I desire." Donna rolled a short section of it out on the picnic table. "Now I'll take this wooden frame and lay it on the canvas like this. Then I'll cut a piece of the canvas that will be about two inches larger than the frame, like this."

"There, you see?" Donna leaned back to give Jen a better view of what she had done. "All cut out and ready to apply to the frame."

"Here's where you need a staple gun. Believe me, it's a lot easier than the tacks my grandmother used to use when she was painting many years ago. She was in the first Allentown Art Festival, you know."

"No, I didn't. Guess that's where you got your talent from."

"Well, my grandmother always said so." Donna laughed.

"Now I'll pull the top center canvas around the frame and staple it to the back like this. See? Then we'll take the bottom center of it and do the same." Donna held the frame up so Jen might see what she was doing. "Then take the center of the side canvas and staple it to the back of the frame, and then the center of the other side. Do you see what I'm doing? We've stretched the canvas into a cross design. All we have to do now is stretch it from one staple to the next and work our way around so it will be evenly stretched. See?"

Donna looked up from her project in time to see the tears spilling down Jen's face.

"Jen! What's wrong?" Donna put the partially stretched frame down and took Jen's hands.

"Nothing." Jen tried to be as stoic as possible, but failed miserably.

"Please, Jen. You can tell me. Something's bothering you. You need to share." Donna forced Jen to face her squarely. "Tell me."

"Oh, Donna." Jen lost control and burst into sobs. "I might be pregnant."

"What?" Donna stared at her and then reached to hug Jen to her.

"Wait a minute." She released Jen from the hug. "You *might* be pregnant? You don't really know?"

Jen couldn't speak. She just shook her head.

"No? Well, Jennifer, the first thing you have to do is to learn if you are or not. Why get yourself sick over something that may not even be a problem?" Donna stood and pulled Jen after her. "Come on. We're going to the drug store and get a pregnancy test. Then we'll weigh our options."

Donna had done the shopping for the test kit since Jen and her family knew the druggist personally. Jen just couldn't face him with this type of purchase.

And now they were home and waiting for the results.

Chapter 17

Vanessa Wilkins was as good a Catholic girl as you could find. She had attended parochial schools, both elementary and high, and finished up with four years at D'Youville College, a Catholic school in Buffalo, where she earned her degree in education. She took first communion at the age of seven and had participated in the weekly ceremony ever since. She had chosen her favorite saint's name, Teresa, as her confirmation name. She personally knew almost all the priests and nuns in her town, and many from near-by ones as well. She attended church every Sunday and observed all the religious holidays, both the popular ones and those more obscure to the average parishioner.

Although her religion surrounded her and made her feel safe and secure, she was not one to push her beliefs on anyone else. She left that to those whose duty it was to do so.

Luckily she had found a mate who shared in her beliefs and they collectively rejoiced in their religious functions. Even though Troy had not attended religious schools, he was still as devout a Catholic as was his wife.

Of course, Jen knew this, and Donna didn't. That's why Donna had no idea what terror she instilled in Jen when she offered her first words of advice.

After watching the color change and both now knowing that Jen was indeed pregnant, Donna solemnly told Jen that the first thing she had to do was let her parents and Vince know. And then, of course, they must discuss it among themselves and come up with the best solution. There were four that Donna could think of, the first one being abortion.

Zing! Right to the heart. Jen actually recoiled, knowing her parents' strong Catholic beliefs. She knew abortion was no option, and she told Donna why. Her parents wouldn't hear of it, and the truth of the matter was, neither could she. Although not as devout or as busy a partaker of the religious rites as her parents, still she was Catholic to the core. She knew that to some people, this early-stage fetus would not be considered a 'life', but because of her strict Catholic upbringing, it was to her. And to abort it, unless it was a case of incest or rape, was tantamount to murder. No, abortion was not an option, and she was sure that Vince, also a good Catholic, would agree with her on that.

"Well, that leaves three," Donna told her.

"Three?" Jen was in a fog of confusion, an eddy swirling round and round. She was losing her bearings and any sense of sane or proper thought.

"Yes, Jen. Three. With abortion out of the picture, you are obviously going to have this baby." Donna stated the obvious.

Jen couldn't believe these words were being directed at

The Secret Monster Within

her. "I'm going to have a baby." She whispered the words, not quite believing them.

Donna gave her a crooked smile. "Yes, sweetie. You are. And that leaves you and Vince three choices, as I've already mentioned."

Jen's blank face said it all.

"You can have the baby and give it up for adoption." Donna took Jen's hand into her own as she saw the look of pain that creased Jen's face. "Or, you can have the baby, and if Vince is still stubborn about not getting married before he has graduated and gotten a good job, it will be up to you and/or your parents to bring the baby up. At least until Vince does agree to marry you."

"What?" Jen looked at her incredulously.

"Or," Donna dragged the last option out, "Vince can do the gentlemanly thing and marry you now. Then you can raise your child together. You may not have the same solid financial beginning to your marriage that he was hoping for, but you'll do what most people do. You'll make do and you'll improve your status as you go along."

"And," she added, "you will both be there, as mother and father, to bring up your child."

***

Vince must be told first. Jen knew that, but how? It was only yesterday that she found out she was pregnant, and she hadn't slept all night. Tossing and turning, her mind ran in a maze of possible ways to present this bombshell news to him, but none of them seemed just right. Actually, she wondered, was there really any right way to say it?

Probably not, she concluded, but was there a better way? She was sure there was, but what was it?

It was Sunday, and she and Vince had been invited to

her parents' house for dinner after church, as was the norm. It would be the perfect opportunity for her to just say "I'm pregnant" to all of them. There, that would take care of it, over and done with by saying just two words. She could envision all three of their faces and knew she couldn't bear it. No, she had to tell Vince first and then they, as a couple, could present it to her parents. She needed an ally. But the big question was, could she count on Vince to take on that role? She wasn't the least bit sure.

She called Vince on his cell, and he answered on the first ring.

"Hi, honey." His voice was full of sleep.

"Hi, handsome." It was a ritual they never veered from.

"What's up?" he asked.

"Well, I have something I'd like to talk to you about. Could you pick me up for church an hour earlier than usual?"

"Sure, hon, but what's so important it can't wait?"

When he received no answer, he asked again, "Give me a clue. What's it all about?" Jen could hear the uncertainty in his voice.

"I'll tell you when you get here. OK?" Jen's voice quivered, and she prayed he would simply agree. No more questions, please. I'm pressured enough.

"OK," he said. "See you soon."

Jen breathed a sigh of relief.

Donna answered the door and Vince noticed that her welcoming smile and hug were warmer and more intense than usual. "Jen's waiting for you upstairs," she said, and then gave him an extra hug.

Vince was baffled and his expression showed it. "Talk to you later," Donna said, and waved him on.

He climbed the stairs with heavy heart. Something was

The Secret Monster Within

wrong, but what could it be?

Jen was waiting for him at the top of the center stairs. She took his hand and led him into her bedroom, and then closed the door.

"All right," he said, "enough of this mystery. What gives?"

"Here, Vince, sit on the love seat with me. I've got something to tell you." Jen sat on the two-seated sofa her parents had given her and patted the space next to her.

Vince sat where she had suggested and turned to look at her. "What is it, Jen?" Jen's worried frown didn't bode well.

"You love me, don't you, Vince?"

"What? Now that's a foolish question. How many times have I told you so?" He seemed to recoil in amazement, but then leaned towards her so he might kiss her lips. "You know I love you. You never have to ask me that. Not ever."

Jen stared into his eyes, and the seconds seemed like minutes, no, like hours. Finally, she sighed and said, "I'm pregnant."

She would never forget the look on his face, the look of terrified horror. "What?" he managed to gasp.

"I'm pregnant." So much for the perfect way to present it.

Vince's blank stare told her nothing. Say something, she kept pleading with her heart, but out loud, she said nothing. She let the two words hang in the air. What else was there to say?

"You're pregnant?" he finally asked.

She nodded, and the tears she had fought to withhold escaped and trickled down her cheeks.

She saw the question in his eyes, and she reminded him of the one time, the one and only time, they had sex without protection. "Damn the luck, eh?"

Vince's face softened and he took her into his arms.

"Oh, honey, I'm so sorry. We'll work this out." But as he said it, he really had no clue as to how.

Vince made an excuse and went into the bathroom. He had to be alone for a few minutes. He was numb and lost in a world of questions and what ifs. How could this have happened? They had always been so careful, so pragmatic about using birth control, and just once, "just once" he whispered to the empty room, they had been remiss. And now, look at the result.

Good God, Jen was pregnant with his baby. All their carefully laid plans had just vanished into the air. Abortion was such an easy solution, although he had trouble picturing it. How do they do it, he wondered? Scrape it out like a D and C? Vacuum it out so it came out in pieces? Ugh. He had read about that and couldn't believe it. Both of them seemed barbaric and cruel to the extreme. And besides, his Catholic upbringing told him that the baby within Jen's body was a living human being. It would be murder to kill it.

He shook his head and wondered how the big "A" question had even entered his head. Of course there would be no abortion. He and Jen would have to own up to their mistake. It wasn't the baby's fault. The baby would live.

***

Vanessa and Troy welcomed both Jen and Vince at the church door with the usual hugs and kisses. "Roast pork today," Donna offered with a smile.

"Sounds great," Vince said through a forced smile. Jen was equally robotic. Vanessa sensed the tension, but decided to save her questions for later, maybe after dinner and

The Secret Monster Within

during desert. Yes, she acknowledged to herself, that was usually the best time for solving problems. She just hoped they hadn't had another fight.

***

Vanessa was disappointed. She had prepared their favorite meal, but neither Jen nor Vince had eaten enough to make it worth the bother.

"I'm sorry," she offered as an apology. "Wasn't it as good as usual?"

"Oh, Mom. Yes. It was delicious." Jen hurried to soothe her mother's concerns. Even though it was just family, her mother always went to a great deal of trouble, making their Sunday repast a true company dinner. They always ate in the small dining room that was just big enough for the six-seated table and the glassed-door buffet that held their best china. The table was always set with the white linen tablecloth and, of course, the good china was used. There was always a salad and hot rolls, an enticing entrée, and something especially delicious for dessert. Her mother could never be faulted for not doing her best to make Sunday a special day with a special dinner. Now Jen felt a wash of guilt as she realized how unresponsive she and Vince had been to all of her mother's efforts.

"It's just," how do I say it, she wondered, "it's just that Vince and I have some disturbing news, and I'm afraid it's taken both of our appetites away."

"What is it, honey?" Her father was pouring his second cup of coffee and tried not to sound as worried as he actually was.

"Mom, Dad." Jen's voice quivered and she took a deep breath to get it under control. "You know Vince and I have been a couple for a long time. You know we love each other and that we plan to marry. It's been a long time in coming, but Vince is going to be graduating soon, and hopes to get a good job soon after."

"Yes, Jen. We know all that. And we think it's a very wise and mature decision on his part." Her father scowled in impatience as he asked, "Why are you bringing it up again?"

Jen looked at Vince, and he nodded his head in a go-ahead sign.

"We're moving the wedding date up." There, that was step number one.

"What?" Both her mother and father spoke as one.

"Why?" Her mother had asked the question she most feared answering.

All the years of a good Catholic upbringing, all the commandments that had been drilled into her head, all the *shalt nots* swirled and bobbed through her brain.

And of course, the ultimate, the red-letter one, *Thou shalt not commit adultery*, now stood out from them all. I've confessed this sin to my priest, along with the fact that I used birth control, but never to my mother or father. How do I tell them? How disappointed will they be in me? What can I do or say to cushion this horrible blow? There were so many questions, but no answers.

Vince came to stand by her side. As he took her hand, he softly said, "Jen and I are going to have a baby."

Why did I ever doubt them, Jen wondered? After the initial shock wore off, her parents came through with hugs and kisses and words of love and comfort. How truly blessed I've been, she thought. She hoped she could be as good a parent to this unknown entity growing inside of her as her mother and father were to her.

The Secret Monster Within

***

"No! She can't be pregnant!" He said it over and over again. It was dawn and he was in the park again, but this time there was no rosy sun, only gray clouds and almost leafless black trees. Now she would really be like her. As much as he hated the thought, he knew in his heart that Jen must die.

Chapter 18

Jen did not want to walk down the aisle with a protruding belly. That would be a blatant in-your-face admission to the congregation of friends and relatives that she was pregnant, and the fact that some of them knew this already and the majority would know soon enough, made no difference to her. No, the wedding plans had to be put in the fast lane and there was so much to do in so little time. Her mother and father helped, but Jen and Vince were in a whirlwind of activity.

Finishing school and being awarded a degree was Number One on the to-do list for Vince and, of course, Jen had a full-time job at Playground for Kids. All the many plans for the wedding had to be pressed into whatever few free minutes each could find. The date was set for one

The Secret Monster Within

month hence. One month of spare moments to plan and execute a full-blown wedding.

And this coming weekend, one of only three before the wedding date, was lost as far as planning was concerned. Vanessa and Troy Wilkins had been told, but there were still Vince's parents and family, all of whom were in the dark as to this momentous occasion. Jen had readily agreed to fly to Boston with Vince Friday night so they might tell them the news in person.

***

Jen was a bundle of nerves. She had met Vince's family a few times before and they had liked her, but that was before they knew she was pregnant with Vince's child. How would they react to this? As much as the Marottis were devout Catholics, they were even more devout Italians. You couldn't find a warmer, more loving family. They wore their emotions on their sleeves and none was afraid to show his or her love for others or their dislike if that should be the case. What would be the case when they learned of this surprise pregnancy and resulting pushed-up wedding?

Vince sensed her worry and took her hand as the plane prepared to land. "It'll be all right, Jen. My family loves you already. They know we plan to marry and they have given their one hundred percent approval of my choice of brides." He squeezed her hand. "We're just moving the date up a bit, that's all. And when my mother finds out she is going to be a grandma for the first time, I'll bet you she will be in seventh heaven. And since you will be the vehicle through which this miracle is about to become a reality, she will love you even more. I promise."

***

"What a lovely surprise!" Vince's mother, Mary Marotti, reached out to hug Jen to her ample bosom. Mary was short, just a bit taller then Jen, but a great deal rounder. She had been a beauty in "her day" as she was wont to call it, but time and too much good Italian food had put the pounds on. After a couple of unsuccessful attempts at a diet, she had given up and accepted her body as it was. She was content and happy to be who she was, and traces of her lost beauty could still be seen.

"We were so happy when you called and told us you were coming to visit us this weekend." Mary's brown eyes sparkled with joy as she hugged Jen again. Jen shyly offered her cheek for a kiss, though she couldn't help but wonder if this might not be the last one that Mary would give her so warmly, so freely.

Vince's father, Joseph, had just released Vince from a welcoming squeeze and turned to Jen. "Come here, Sweetie. Give an old man a hug," he said as he opened his arms to welcome her. He was almost as tall as Vince, but had acquired a rotund belly that broadcast to the world how much he enjoyed his wife's cooking.

Again, Jen wondered just how welcoming would be those arms when he learned the reason they were here.

***

Jen loved Italian food, and no one could cook it any better than Vince's mother. "What a wonderful meal, Mary," Jen said, while licking the fork clean. No acting needed, as she meant it from the bottom of her heart.

"Amen." Vince's brother, Angelo, raised his glass of wine in a means of agreement. He was two years older than Vince, but had no plans to marry. "You see, Mom," he said, "if you didn't cook this good, maybe I would have found

The Secret Monster Within

myself a bride and settled down with her. But how can I leave such a delicious cuisine? It's all your fault." He laughed heartily, as did everyone else.

Vince's three sisters, all of them younger than he, laughed too.

"Hey, what are you laughing at, Lori?" Mary pointed her finger at her eldest daughter. "Vince, did you know your sister has found that Mr. Someone?"

"No," Vince acknowledged, with raised eyebrows. "Tell me about him, Sis."

"His name is Mike, and he's tall, dark and handsome, just like you, Vinnie." Lori threw him a kiss. "I wouldn't settle for anything less, you know."

"Well, I should hope not." Vince returned her air-blown kiss.

"He's got a job in sales, and is already making a good living. He's asked me to marry him and I've agreed. We haven't set a wedding date yet though." Lori Anne Marotti's face glowed with love and happiness.

Vince got up and put his arm around his sister's shoulders and gave her a kiss on the cheek. "I'm so happy for you, Sis. That's really great news."

"Thanks," she replied shyly.

Jen closed her eyes and realized that now their news would present a double whammy. Lori was planning on being the first bride in her family and more than likely the mother of their first grandchild, but now she was about to be put in second place on both scores. She'll hate us for stealing her thunder, Jen thought. Oh God. Oh God. How are we going to do this?

Vince retained his cool, calm demeanor. He continued smiling while he sat down and turned to his second youngest sister. "And how about you, Addie?"

"Hey, I'm just starting college. I'm going to become a

nurse before I become a Mrs."

Adelaide Marotti was a no-nonsense type of girl who had set her sights on being a nurse at the early age of eight and had never veered off track. This was her destiny, and everyone in the family knew it, including Vince.

He smiled because he knew her answer even before she gave it. "Good for you, my beauteous one." Vince made an OK sign with his fingers and turned to his last sibling. "And you?" he drawled.

"Well, I thought I might finish high school first." Sixteen-year-old Valerie laughed.

"And you darn well better." Her father pretended to scowl at her.

Jen loved this family. They had so much heart, so much love for each other. How she dreaded the possibility that all of this could evaporate when they heard their news. If only, she thought. If only.

After dinner and dessert were finished and everyone was enjoying their second cup of coffee, Vince stood up from the table and all eyes were upon him. Jen's stomach roiled because she knew what was coming.

Vince cleared his throat. "Jen and I have some news we'd like to share with you." The raucous noise subsided and there was complete silence. Jen had to fight to keep the tears from overflowing. Don't cry she admonished herself and she bit her lip in an effort to stop the flow, but it didn't help. The tears were welling.

Vince took Jen's hand and signaled her to stand beside him. "As you all know, Jen and I have been a two-some for some time now. You also know we've planned to marry in the near future. What you don't know, is just how near that future is."

"What?" Joseph asked the question and almost spilled

The Secret Monster Within

his cup of coffee.

"I hope you are all free four weeks from today. That is, if you want to attend our wedding." Vince hugged Jen to him. She put her arm around his waist and stared with frightened eyes at his family.

"What?" Everyone asked the question this time.

Vince swallowed hard and squared his shoulders as if to do battle. There was a moment when no one said a word, but then the silence was broken by a cacophony of voices, everyone seeking answers at once.

Vince put his hand up in an effort to stem the questions.

"You need only one answer." Vince turned to his parents. "Mom. Dad. How do you feel about becoming grandparents?"

"What?"

"I love Jen, and she is pregnant with my baby." There, it was said. The moment he was dreading was over and done with, and now there was nothing left to do but live with the results. "I hope you all wish us well." Vince heard Jen's thin cry escape her closed lips, and he hugged her even tighter.

Again, everyone sat is stunned silence with gaping mouths.

Then Mary Marotti rose from her seat and motioned for Jen to come closer.

"Jen." Mary's face was a blank slate. "Come here." Jen looked at Vince for reassurance then took a tentative step toward Vince's mother.

"Come here," Mary insisted with firm voice.

The short walk felt like a mile, and now here she was, in front of Vince's mother. Jen held her breath, not knowing if she would receive a slap on the face or a torrent of accusations. Instead, Mary hugged her tightly. And then she leaned back and smiled at Jen. "I'm going to be a grandmother?"

"Yes," Jen whispered.

"YES!" Mary shouted. "Yes, yes, yes."

The whole family rose as one to embrace Vince and Jen, even Lori, whose thunder they had stolen.

***

It had been a wonderful weekend, and now Jen leaned her head on Vince's shoulder as the plane leveled off on their trip home. "How lucky I am, Vince. I love your family."

"And they love you." Vince kissed his fiancé.

***

Time was marching on, and he knew what he had to do. But Jen? Dear sweet Jen? How he dreaded it, but he knew in his heart he couldn't bear to see her with a baby. It would remind him of her and it would be too much for him to handle. He had time, but it must be done before the baby was born. It just had to be.

Chapter 19

Jennifer Wilkins was no different from any other young girl. She had been dreaming of her wedding day ever since she was old enough to know she could have one. Of course, like all other little girls, her dreams and desires had changed through the years. The cut of her gown had metamorphosed from a princess style hoop to that of a sophisticated, short-trained beauty. The music that would accompany her walk down the aisle had gone from Lohengrin's Wedding March to one of the Beatles' lovely songs, and then back to the Wedding March again. Her childhood friend, Patty Stark would be her maid of honor, but Patty Stark had moved away years ago. There would be vast arrays of foods, and fountains of drinks, mostly champagne, but now, as an adult, she gasped when she saw the cost of even a minimal offering. Oh, yes, dreams change as you age, but one thing remained a constant. Never could she imagine being married inside a church or celebrating a reception inside a hall. No, never.

She always knew she would be married outside on a lovely summer's day when the sky would be the bluest of blue and there would be little puffs of clouds in stark contrast. All the flowers and foliage would be in full bloom and the essence of roses would waft through the air. Never had this vision changed.

Now she stared out the window and saw the raw wind blowing the dried up leaves, and knew that her dream would remain just that.

"Did you mail the invitations, honey?" Vanessa came up from behind her and put her arm around her daughter's waist.

Jen turned and smiled at her mother. "Yep. Got them out this morning. I hope all our friends and relatives can make it on such short notice."

"I'm sure people will work it out. They won't want to miss your big day." Vanessa gave her daughter a little hug and turned to sit at the desk. "Let's go over the list and see what we have left to do. OK?"

"OK." Jen was all smiles as she pulled up a chair and sat next to her mother.

"We've lined up the church for the rehearsal and the wedding date with Father Sullivan. You said you have taken care of the flowers, right?" Vanessa turned to look at her daughter for affirmation.

"Yes, it's all done. I told you the cost. Now where is the quote?" Jen looked through a pile of papers resting on the over-crowded desk. "Oh, here it is." She handed it to her mother. "I know it's fall, but I really want roses, red, pink and white. I'm missing my outside wedding, but I just

The Secret Monster Within

couldn't give up on the roses."

Vanessa patted her daughter's hand. "And you don't have to, honey. Roses will be lovely."

"Thanks, Mom."

"Salvatores has been reserved for the reception." Vanessa closed her eyes in a form of prayerful thanks. "Russ gave us a good price, but then, your dad and he have been friends for years. What a classy guy Russ is, and what a beautiful place to have your wedding reception."

"If it can't be outside, it will be he next best thing," Jen acknowledged.

"Oh," Jen continued with enthusiasm, "I forgot to tell you some good news. Vince's good friend, Todd March, is an up-and-coming photographer. I know he's just starting out, but Vince has shown me some of his work and it's beautiful, so we've agreed to have him as our official photographer. Here, look." Jen handed her mother the handwritten quote.

"Wow." Vanessa raised her eyebrows in a sign of astonishment. "If you and Vince like his work, I'm sure we will," Vanessa assured her daughter. "And I really like the look of that very reasonable price." She smiled at the unexpected bargain.

"And speaking of good news," she continued, "I've got some too. Mary Marotti called and said they will take care of all the liquid refreshments. That will be one expense we don't have to worry about. And she sounded so nice."

"Oh, Mom, she is. You'll love her and his whole family. I can't wait for you to meet them."

"I'm looking forward to it too."

"Oh," Vanessa had another thought. "You'll take care of the band, right? I have no idea where to begin."

"Vince is working on that, Mom. He's got to get involved in this too."

"I'm all for that."

Vanessa took Jen's hands once more. "Honey, I can't believe you are going to get married and have a baby. You've been my little girl for so long."

"I can hardly believe it myself, Mom. And I can't thank you enough for all the support and help you've given me ever since we told you. I don't know what I would have done if you had turned your back on me."

"Honey! Your dad and I will never turn our backs on you. We love you with all our hearts." Vanessa leaned over and pressed her cheek against her daughter's. "You'll make a beautiful bride and a wonderful mother. I can hardly wait to meet our grandchild."

"Me neither." Jennifer rubbed her stomach, and she and her mother shared a joyful laugh.

***

He could see Jen's face, interposed upon that of hers. They were so much alike. They had the same coloring, the same tiny body, the same round breasts, the same dark curly hair, the same, the same, the same. They were so much alike. And now, she was pregnant, just as she had been. He had loved her, and he loved Jen. But what was he to do? The Monster within him told him exactly what he was to do.

No. No. No. I'll find someone else, he told the Monster. I'll find lots of others. That should satisfy The Monster. Just not Jen. Please, not Jen.

Chapter 20

Nadine Westerbrook checked to make sure that everything was cleaned up, shut off, and put away. Her boss, the owner of Kathy's Korner, had lost her temper when she came to work one morning and found that Nadine had left the burner on under the chili container. The chili had cooked away and dried into a black crust, but luckily, LUCKILY, she had shouted, it hadn't started a fire. It could have though. Did Nadine understand that?

Well, if she didn't, she sure did now. Nadine checked once more, just to make sure.

"Everything's off," she informed her absent boss.

She looked at the clock that was over the register. Going on midnight again. Her hours were listed as three to eleven, but by the time she had said goodbye to the last customer, and had cleaned up, it was always closer to midnight before she left. That's almost an hour I don't get paid for. An hour I have to pay a babysitter for. Her temper waned as she thought of her sweet baby waiting for her at home.

She and Dave had been an item through all four years of high school. She still couldn't believe that he had turned tail and run when he found out she was pregnant. Four years of sweet talk and promises, none of which came true.

But she didn't care. She had a beautiful one-year-old baby boy. She was the one who had garnered the best of it. I don't know where you are, Dave, and I don't give a damn. Just don't ever come home and think you will be part of this family. She told him this over and over again in her head, but in her heart she knew if he came back, she would welcome him with open arms. What fools we women are, she would chastise herself. It seemed easier to class her foibles along with all of women-kind rather than accept it for herself alone.

She checked the front door to make sure it was locked and left the few lights on that Kathy Turner had told her to. "Creeps won't be so quick to rob us when they have to do so in the light." A lot of Kathy was irritating, but she had to agree with her on this. Nadine left via the back door and walked to her car, the only one left in the dimly lit parking lot.

She had her keys out. Dave had repeatedly told her to always lock her car door and, equally important, always have her keys ready and in your hands when you come back to your car. Don't spend time in a parking lot searching for them in your purse or pocket he had admonished, and he went on to emphasize how much this made you a sitting duck for anyone lurking near-by. Besides, a key between the second and third finger of a fist made for a won-

The Secret Monster Within

derful weapon. Always aim for the juggler or the eyes he had told her.

"Darn it!" she exclaimed. "Did I leave the car door unlocked again. I could have sworn I locked it." She scolded herself for letting number one on Dave's list slip. Where is my brain, she wondered as she opened the car door and slipped into the front seat? She hadn't found the ignition yet, when someone sitting in the back seat found her throat instead.

***

Was that enough, Monster? Or do you want another? Just not Jen. Please, please. Not Jen.

Chapter 21

"What a glorious day for your wedding." Vanessa turned from the window to look at her daughter. "Look at that sky." She pulled the drapes back for better viewing. "And it's so nice and warm. Don't you just love these Indian Summers?"

"Well, somebody up there must like me." Jen walked to the window to share the view with her mother. "It's been so dreary and cold lately, but this day must be my wedding gift from God." Jen raised her head and closed her eyes in a silent form of thanks.

It was a short thank-you though as a thought occurred to her. "Hey," she wailed, "we could have had my wedding outside if we had known it would be like this." Jen feigned a look of disappointment, but she could only hold it for a

The Secret Monster Within

moment. She brightened as her mother held up her wedding gown.

"Oooo," she said with pursed lips, and her mother was quick to agree.

"Honey, I just love this dress," Vanessa told her for what seemed to be the hundredth time.

"Me, too. I was so lucky to find it." Jen fingered the white satin bodice that was embroidered with seed pearls and sequins, and then turned it around to check the short round train that was similarly decorated.

"A beautiful day, a beautiful gown, and a beautiful bride. I would say this bodes well for my soon-to-be-wed daughter." Vanessa kissed Jen on the cheek. "Oh, and a beautiful baby on the way."

"And no more morning sickness!" Jen held her hands over her thickening stomach and raised her eyes in thanks once more. "Somebody up there *does* like me."

***

St. Mary's was a medium sized church, not too big and not too small, but large enough to hold the many relatives and friends whom wanted to share in the joy of Jen and Vince's wedding. The stained glass windows provided an instrument for the sun to shed a kaleidoscope of jewel-like colors throughout the church, and the three-stories-high arched white ceilings created a feeling of majesty.

The altar was bedecked with bouquets of pink and white roses that peeked through froths of baby's breath and greenery, and their sweet aroma wafted throughout the church. Only the background organ music lent a touch of solemnity to the otherwise festive atmosphere.

Vince stood at the altar with his best friend, George Carpenter, who had readily agreed to be his best man. Both they and the ushers were resplendent in their black tuxes, white ruffled shirts, and red cummerbunds.

Everyone in the church turned as one when the organ music changed to The Wedding March and they saw Vince's little cousin, Annabelle Latona, solemnly lead the bridal procession. How she loved her long multi-colored gown of black, white, gray and pink stripes, and it was only through sheer will power that she was able to resist the urge to skip and twirl so she might better show it off. Her tiny hand reached into the ribbon-bedecked basket she held on her other wrist to gather the pink rose petals that she scattered on the white runner that covered the center aisle.

At eight years of age, she was taking her duties very seriously. Everyone smiled as she passed their pew, but because of her concentrated effort, she missed all the happy faces. Having been told more than once what an honor it was to serve as a flower girl in a wedding ceremony, she was determined to do it right, so she never raised her eyes from her assigned duty. The petals were distributed just so.

Following Annabelle were Jen's bridesmaids and maid of honor. The guests emitted a communal sound of approval as they watched the bridal party approach. The color scheme was stunning. Jewel Johnson, the maid of honor, wore a sleek halter-type gown of black satin that featured a stunning diagonal slash of white, while the two bridesmaids each wore an identical style, only in a soft dove gray. Each carried a small bouquet of pink roses that were nested in a bed of greenery. The combination of black and white, and pink and gray caused everyone to gasp and whisper their approval to the one sitting next to them.

And then there was Jen, and never had she looked more beautiful. Her too-curly hair was pulled back into a cluster that was adorned with a short halo-type veil. The wedding gown that she and her mother both adored drew rave re-

The Secret Monster Within

views from all the guests. Jen was short, but the high heels and the cut of the gown gave her added height and, as she had been only too happy to point out to her mother, did a good job of hiding her thickening tummy. The sparkling jewels on her ears and bodice came in second to the radiance that glowed from her happy face.

Vanessa and Troy Wilkins proudly walked on either side of her, and Vanessa hoped that everyone would know that the tears in her eyes were tears of joy. All three smiled broadly at the guests, even nodding and throwing air kisses to some.

When they reached the altar, Jen kissed both her parents and whispered "I love you" to each of them and they whispered the same sentiment back to her. She held the large bouquet of red roses in her left arm, and extended her right hand to Vince who seemed to be awe-struck at the overwhelming beauty of his bride-to-be. He shook his head and smiled at her as he drew her to his side. Vanessa and Troy walked to their front-row seats, and the ceremony began.

The priest recited the ritualistic words, and Jen felt as though she was in a world of make-believe. She had been dreaming of this day all her life and now it was here. It was actually here. She was being married, and to one she could not love more.

When it came to giving their vows, each had prepared a short one that came straight from their hearts. Jen swore to be by her husband's side, through thick and thin, through the good times and the bad. She avowed her love for him and swore nothing, absolutely nothing would ever change it. Vince, in turn, vowed to love, respect and cherish her as long as she might live, and prophesied all of the happy days they had ahead of them as husband and wife.

Vince took her hand and turned to look into her eyes. His look was so intense that it almost gave her chills.

Margaret McMillen

***

"May I present Mr. and Mrs. Vince Marotti." George Carpenter stood and raised his glass when Jen and Vince arrived at the reserved banquet hall at Salvatore's Restaurant. The guests stood as one and applauded the newlywed couple, and Jen and Vince responded with smiles that lit up the room.

Salvatores was a classic example of over-doneness that turned out just right. The huge carpeted banquet rooms were each highlighted with three-story-high ceilings, each adorned with massive crystal chandeliers. Floor to ceiling pillars added to the majesty and to embellish the ambiance even more, the whole restaurant was filled with works of statuary art, both large and small, that would make any museum green with envy. It was elegance personified.

Jen was an only child, and as such, nothing was spared to make it a perfect day. It wasn't outdoors but almost all her other dreams came true. Two white linen tables were laden with delicious hors d'oeuvres, and there were gold fountains of champagne surrounded by long-stemmed crystal ware. A violinist walked among the guests while playing soft melodies. Each table was adorned with low bouquets of roses, greenery and baby's breath. The word *beautiful* was repeated over and over again.

And dinner lived up to everyone's high expectations. Shrimp cocktails were served first, followed by a Caesar salad and hot bread. Steak ala Russell, Russell Salvatore's signature entrée, lived up to its delicious reputation and was complimented by side dishes of twice-baked potatoes, and roasted vegetables. The meal was followed by a lemon sorbet.

And then it was time to cut the three-tiered wedding cake. It was half-chocolate and half-white, hopefully ac-

The Secret Monster Within

commodating everyone's taste, with the usual white frosting. But Jen didn't want white roses. No, they had to be pink, very pale pink she had insisted, with very pale green leaves.

And it was everything she had hoped for. "Andre, the baker, is a true artist," she exclaimed in awe. "How truly beautiful it is." The cake was a masterpiece of art with roses and scallops and twists and twirls. The top layer was adorned with a bride and groom that held hands under an arbor of pink roses.

Jen and Vince posed with the knife and cut the first piece. The flashing bulbs from Todd March's camera were almost blinding, but Jen knew how much she would treasure these pictures in years to come. It was, indeed, her fairy-tale wedding come true.

***

He saw her beautiful face all aglow and pictured the life draining from it. It would kill him. No, monster. I can't, I can't. But The Monster's voice kept telling him, "You must. You must."

Chapter 22

Bernie Roper turned the TV off with a flick of the remote. He balled his hands up into two fists, and smashed them against the top of the coffee table in front of him. "Damn, damn, damn!" he muttered through clenched teeth. The news was the same—the same as yesterday and probably the same as tomorrow, more murders and no clues. The Monster was mocking them, making fools of them, making it a game, a game where no one won except The Monster. And some, those beautiful young girls, were losing so much.

"One lucky break, God. Please, just one lucky break." Bernie wasn't all that religious, but there were times, like now, when there seemed to be nothing else to do but pray.

The Secret Monster Within

***

"Can you believe it? Thanksgiving is just around the corner. Wasn't it summer last week?" Bernie shook his head at how fast time was flying.

"It sure seems that way, doesn't it?" Dan smiled at his friend. "But I'm really looking forward to this holiday."

"Yeah? How come? Got a hot date?"

"Don't know if I'd call it hot but it's a very special one for me. My son, Drew, is coming to stay with me for the four-day weekend." Dan's smile broadened into a big grin.

"Hey. That's great." Bernie gave Dan a knuckle jab in the arm. "How come?"

"Well, Brenda and George are going on a cruise, and Drew didn't want to go. He asked if he could stay with me, and Brenda most graciously agreed, if I would have him."

"Ha," Dan scoffed. "If I would have him? Is she kidding? I miss my son. I get to see him now and then, but to have him for four whole days.... Well, it's something I'm really looking forward to. I'm really going to have something to be thankful for this holiday."

"Dan, that's just great. Happy for you, buddy. I hope you put in for some time off so you can do some things with him." Bernie raised his eyebrows so Dan would know that although presented as a statement, it deserved an answer.

"You'd better believe it. As soon as I found out, I got that Friday off. Now all I have to do is figure out where and what we'll eat on Thanksgiving. Neither one of us can cook." Dan laughed. "Thank God for restaurants."

"Well, that's where I go every Thanksgiving." Bernie tried to downplay the hollow sound of it.

"You know, I never thought of that. You don't have any family here, Bernie?"

"Just me, myself and I. The three of us are great company."

"Well, there'll be five of us this year then. The three of you--you, yourself and you, and Drew and me. What do you think of that? Of course, if yourself and you can't come, then just you...oh, wait a minute, I mean if me, myself and I can't come, then just I...wait a minute. " Dan got into a laughing jag. "Well, anyway" he said after drawing a ragged breath, " there'll be three of us. No one needs to be lonesome on Thanksgiving Day."

"You sure?" Bernie looked at him with questioning eyes.

"You bet your sweet ass I am. We'll be three bachelors out on the town, on Thanksgiving Thursday. Watch out, town." Dan scowled and then laughed. "It'll be fun," he promised.

"I'm looking forward to it. Thanks for including me." Bernie rose to shake his friend's hand.

"Anytime, buddy. Anytime."

***

Because it had been such a short time since their last visit, Ken and Maureen felt doubly blessed when they learned that their daughter, son-in-law and granddaughter were going to be able to visit them over the Thanksgiving holidays after all. Kyle had explained that even though Terry was fairly new on the job, he had been offered this November holiday if he would agree to work through the Christmas one. He and his family had been only too happy to comply.

Ken and Maureen would have loved having the whole family together during the most sacred holiday of all, but they knowingly admitted that December 25 was a bad time

The Secret Monster Within

to make plans for traveling to Buffalo. Just last year, a whopping snowstorm had closed the Buffalo airport for three days, and so Kyle's family had been unable to make the trip that they had been so eagerly looking forward to. Poor Kyle had bought nothing for the holiday dinner since she was planning on being in Buffalo for Christmas, so as it was, they had to jump shift and make do with what they had on hand. Kyle cried on the phone and told Maureen it was the worst holiday she had ever had. No, Maureen didn't want to put her daughter through that again.

So Thanksgiving was a pleasant substitute. Not that Thanksgiving was a given, mind you, but it certainly offered better odds. Maureen and Ken could remember a few white Thanksgiving holidays, but it was rare, and even then, the snow was usually just a light covering, nothing that would close an airport down.

"I'd say we're lucky you got Thanksgiving off," she informed her son-in-law with a laugh, and he, a thoroughbred southern boy, readily agreed.

No one need question who Rachel's father was. His bright red hair, green eyes, and freckled face told it all.

***

Bernie Roper rang the bell at Dan Halloway's apartment. The door was opened with great fanfare, and Bernie had to laugh as Dan bowed a royal welcome.

"Come in, and welcome," Dan said with great majesty.

"Why, thank you, kind sir." It was easy for Bernie to get into the holiday spirit since this was a rare one indeed, one in which he would not be alone.

He bowed in response, and offered Dan the expensive bottle of wine he had brought.

"Hey," Dan said as he examined the label, "this is the

good stuff. You are hereby ordered to come every Thanksgiving from now on. I can't afford this."

"The least I could do," Bernie said with a smile and a shoulder shrug.

Dan and his son had talked it over and decided that eating out just didn't cut it for a holiday as special as Thanksgiving, so both cautiously agreed it was time they learned how to make a holiday meal. They poured over cookbooks and approached every housewife they knew, including Brenda, seeking answers to the mystery of cooking a turkey.

"Well," Dan grimaced, then laughed at Ben, "you know you are our guinea pig. Cooking a meal like this is a first for both Drew and me. Hope you don't mind."

"Mind? Are you kidding?" Bernie joined in Dan's laughter. "Just being with someone for a holiday meal is a real treat for me. I don't care how it turns out! Believe me when I say that."

"That's good. Here, let me have your coat." Dan put the wine down and helped Bernie out of his all-weather outerwear. "I want you to meet my son. Come on in." Dan picked up the wine and motioned Bernie into his living room.

"Hey, Drew," Dan shouted to the kitchen door. "Leave the turkey for a minute. Got someone here I want you to get to know."

At that, a Greek God appeared in the kitchen doorway.

"Wow," Bernie said. "This is your son? What's he doing here? Shouldn't he be in Hollywood?"

Drew chuckled. "That's what I keep telling Dad but then he brings me right back to earth." Both father and son laughed.

"Well, if anybody could do it, it would be you."

"Thank you, Chief Roper."

"Call me Bernie, please." Bernie took Drew's offered hand. "But I do appreciate the sign of respect. Too many young ones have forgotten how to do that."

"I've got me a good kid." Dan put his arm around his son's broad shoulders.

"You are one lucky fellow." Bernie felt a pang in the pit of his stomach for having missed out on so much.

"That I am." Dan smiled at his son. "But as handsome as he is, he still has to baste the turkey."

Drew made a face and then smiled as he returned to the kitchen.

"Would you mind pouring us some wine, Bernie? I've got to check on the potatoes and squash. There are some wine glasses in that buffet." Dan indicated which one with a nod of his head.

"I'd love to," Bernie said. He was enjoying this warm feeling of camaraderie and wondered how he could ever repay Dan.

The best he could do at this point was offer a toast when their wine glasses had been filled. "Thank you, dear friend, for inviting me to share this holiday with you and your son. It is one of the best ones I've had in years."

"And you have added equally to ours, hasn't he, Drew?" Dan raised his glass in response.

"You most certainly have, Bernie." Drew raised his glass as well.

Three men, sharing a Thanksgiving holiday, each one making it better for the other.

***

Vanessa and Troy were delirious with joy on this Thanksgiving Day. It would be the first holiday that their newly married daughter and their brand new son-in-law would join them.

"Mr. and Mrs. Marotti! Welcome!" A rush of cold air

accompanied Jen and Vince as they entered the Wilkin's home for the first time since they had returned from their honeymoon. Even though the newly-weds had been home for over a week, they knew they would be together with the Wilkins on the holiday so they saw no need to rush a visit. A couple of phone calls should suffice.

Or so Jen thought. Vanessa ground her teeth and did all she could to maintain her poise and proper demeanor. You just wait till you have a daughter who goes away on a honeymoon, and doesn't bother to come see you for days after she returns. You just wait and see how that makes you feel. This scolding was all in Vanessa's head, of course, and never verbalized, but it was there nevertheless.

"Hi, Mom." Jen looked pink and white from the cold air.

"Hi, Mom." Vince choked on the title, but knew in his heart that it had to become as natural as when he addressed his own mother. Vanessa had made it very clear to her new son-in-law that she and Troy were to be addressed as Mom and Dad. And, as difficult as it was to use the title of Mom on Vanessa, it proved to be even harder when he greeted Troy. "Hi, Dad." His voice cracked like that of an adolescent.

"Oh, my sweeties." Vanessa was so happy to see them that their selfish act of thoughtlessness was forgiven right then and there.

Hugs and kisses were exchanged by all.

"Um. Something sure smells good." Vince was making points, although it wasn't difficult to say since something really did smell good.

"Ham and turkey, two small ones. Your choice, or both." Troy helped Vince out of his coat, and hung it in the front closet with the rest of them.

"Come sit on the sofa and tell us about your honey-

The Secret Monster Within

moon." Troy motioned them both into the family room. Jen and Vince held hands as they walked into the cozy room and continued to do so as they sat on the soft upholstered couch.

"Well," Jen said, "as you know, we rented a condo right on the beach. There was only a small strip of sand between our condo and the ocean, and our bedroom was in front so you could hear the waves breaking against the shore. Umm." Jen briefly closed her eyes and rocked back and forth as she relived the soft sounds of the waves. "It would lull me to sleep. In fact," she said as she opened her eyes and continued with enthusiasm, "we loved the sound so much that we searched and found a recording of white noise that mimics the sound of the ocean, so now we have brought a bit of Myrtle Beach back to Buffalo." She chuckled and winked at Vince. He squeezed her hand and smiled back at her.

"As you know," Vince said, "the Caribbean was our first choice, but since this was the hurricane season, we didn't want to take any chances. So Myrtle Beach it was. And it was wonderful there. Still fairly warm, and we loved walking the beach and picking up seashells."

Vanessa gleamed with pleasure. "I'm so glad you liked it since it was our suggestion. We've been to Myrtle Beach so many times, haven't we, Troy?" Vanessa looked at her husband with a smile as they remembered the many March's they had spent there together.

"You bet." Troy grinned at his wife. "And we loved being there. We used to enjoy the live shows, though we hear they've cut down on them a bit." He shrugged. "Nevertheless, the weather is good and there are plenty of other things to do. So what did you two find to do?"

"Well," Jen drawled as she put her mind to it, "we did go to a couple of the less expensive shows. And we ate out a lot." Both Jen and Vince laughed when she said that since they both knew Jen was as far from the natural homemaker as you could get. In fact, she was lucky if she could fry an egg without breaking it. Troy and Vanessa joined in the laughter since this was not news to them either.

"And we walked the beach every day. Sometimes, twice a day."

"We went shopping." Jen felt a need to add to the list. "Pretty much just window shopping, of course, since we aren't exactly swimming in the green stuff," she added with a laugh.

"And we just goofed off." Vince figured that should do it.

"And that's what vacations and honeymoons, are for." Vanessa rose to attend to her chores in the kitchen.

"Can I help, Mom?" Jen had decided it was time to learn some of the cooking hints her mother had heretofore not bothered to share with her.

"Why, sure, honey. I could use some for the last-minute things. Thanks." Vanessa beamed her gratitude.

"What a happy Thanksgiving this is." Vanessa hugged her daughter and took her hand as she went into the kitchen.

***

The honeymoon is over. The monster kept reminding him of that. Time marches on, and she is getting more and more pregnant by the day. Her time is coming soon.

"No, no. Not Jen! No, no, no" he cried softly to himself as he turned his face into the pillow. Then he peeked to see if his wife had heard. He was relieved to see she was sleeping soundly.

"Yes, yes, yes." That's all the monster would say.

Chapter 23

Sharon Kelly was the proverbial life of the party, the type you could always count on for laughs. But, as the old saying goes, you can't judge a book by its cover. All the outward froth and frivolity hid a core of steel, and those who knew her well soon learned she was no patsy. Just ask Tom Kenton. He could tell you.

The fledgling Acme Company had hired both Tom and Sharon within one week of each other. Tom, who was tall, brawny, and self-assured, dismissed his competition as too insignificant to worry about. Sharon was petty enough, but much too frivolous to take seriously. He knew he could outdo her in sales with practically no effort on his part. If only one was to survive and progress up the corporate ladder, it would be Tom. There was no doubt about it, none at all.

Acme served as a middleman. If your company needed something printed, you could count on Acme to get it done, and it would be done right, or as their too cute slogan exclaimed, "Acme done write!" Of course they were to be paid for this service, and it was Tom and Sharon's job to find more of these willing-to-pay-customers.

Tom had a young bride and a brand new baby. The hours on the road proved to be tough on him and his family, but it was something they agreed was worthwhile. There would be promotions down the line and these tortuous days of his being away from his family would be but a distant memory. It was just a phase they had to live through because they knew in their hearts that better days were coming.

Sharon, on the other hand, was single and free as a bird. The days on the road were an adventure, and she had no one to answer to except her immediate boss, and he liked Sharon a lot. Actually, more than he should.

Richard Barker had been quite the lothario in his younger days, and he had retained his striking good looks through the years so that even now, at fifty, he caught the eye of most women. Good looks or not, he was a married man with three grown children, and his not-so-subtle advances were most unwelcome. Ordinarily Sharon would have had no trouble putting him in his place, but Richard was her boss, and she desperately needed this job. Talk about being between a rock and a hard place.

Being on the road was a welcome escape. She loved it, and her sales figures began going off the charts. Tom was just now beginning to realize what a true competitor she was.

She flew home every Friday night and went directly to her office to sum up her week's work. It was a good time to get her paper work done since there was no one there on

The Secret Monster Within

Friday night other than Bill Walkerman, the janitor who always greeted her with a warm welcome.

Tonight was no exception. He peeked into the office she shared with an absent-now Tom and greeted her with a warm smile. "Hi, Sharon. Good week?"

"The best week ever!" Sharon raised her hand in an OK sign, and returned his smile. "How are you doing, Bill?"

"Just fine, thanks. The Mrs. and I are going on vacation next week. You'll have to get used to a new face. Only for a week though," he added quickly lest she think he was being replaced.

"Oh, how nice. Where are you going? Anyplace special?"

"We're going to visit our son in Florida. Port Charlotte, actually. Looking forward to some warm, sunny weather."

"You can certainly feel Mr. Winter's breath here now, can't you?" Sharon wrapped her arms around herself and shivered. "It won't be long before we see some snow. Good time to visit down south." Sharon smiled with a nod that indicated the conversation had lasted long enough.

Bill returned the nod. "Sure is," he agreed. "See you a week from Monday."

"Looking forward to it. You can tell me all about your vacation then."

"You got it." Bill signaled with a small salute and continued on his way.

Sharon returned to the paper work that would take more time than usual since she had secured a brand new account. She was bursting at the seams with feelings of elation, and desperately needed someone with whom to share this joy. She felt like a volcano on the verge of eruption, and her hands shook as she punched in the phone card numbers.

The phone was answered on the first ring and she heard her mother's voice responding with a polite "Hello."

"Mom! Hi. It's Sharon. Guess what."

"Oh, honey, what a nice surprise. What is it?"

"I'm so excited, I couldn't wait to share." Sharon squeezed her eyes shut and took a deep breath. "I just landed the biggest account this company has ever had!"

"What? Oh, honey, I'm so happy for you. And proud, too."

Sharon knew her mother had no idea what those words meant to her. Her mother loved all three of her children with the same deep intensity, never favoring one over the other, but in spite of this incomparable love, Sharon had always felt a distant third. Both of her brothers had inherited all the brains. Bruce was a full-fledged lawyer, passing the bar with no problem, and Gary was doing so well as a senior resident surgeon that he had already garnered offers of a position from more than one hospital. Sharon, on the other hand, had always passed, but never with honors.

She had decided nursing was her calling and attended college for one year before realizing she couldn't stand the sight of blood. She had switched to Buffalo State College for a degree in education before she acknowledged she couldn't bear the thought of spending a lifetime in a classroom filled with little children. "Let's face it," she had told her parents, "children have never been my favorite group of people." They were kind enough not to suggest that this was something she might have thought about before going for a teaching degree.

Then she had done the only thing left for her to do, and that was to quit college and spend time *finding herself*, an act that was getting to be more and more the norm. In order to get by, she had answered an ad that required some degree of selling ability, and that's when her personality came to the fore. She had found her niche, and here she was, earning some much-desired accolades from her mother.

The Secret Monster Within

"Thanks, Mom. I just couldn't wait to share this bonanza with someone."

"Well, I'm certainly glad you picked me. Looks like you are really going places, and I'm so happy for you. Oh, how I wish I could give you a congratulatory hug. I hate you being so far away." Sharon could hear the tonal pout.

"I miss you too, Mom."

"Well then, when are you coming here for a visit? I'll bet it's getting cold up there, and you know it's nice and warm here in Orlando."

"That sounds especially good today. It's really blustery." Sharon heard the wind howl through the cracks in her office window. Better make sure Bill weatherproofs that for the winter.

"Well, there you have it. Come on down to toasty Florida. Do you realize it's been over six months since we've seen you?"

"I know, Mom. I miss you so much." She was still reeling from her parents' decision to move to Florida a little over a year ago. "Maybe when they see this new account, I'll have some bargaining power and then I can ask for a week off. It's worth a try. I'll let you know, OK?"

"Ok, sweetie. Call me Monday night. I can't wait to hear what your boss has to say when he hears the good news of your outstanding sale."

"You've got it, Mom. Talk to you then." Sharon paused as she thought of her far-away family. "I guess Dad's at Rotary meeting tonight, right?"

"Oh, you know your dad. Wouldn't miss that one."

"Well, tell him the good news. I'll call Monday and talk to you both then."

"All right, honey. Have a good weekend. I love you."

"You too. Bye."

Sharon smiled as she placed the phone back on its cradle.

Margaret McMillen

It was late when she finished her paper work and she toyed with the idea of skipping The Club all together, but was quick enough to disregard such an outlandish idea. Not one of her group of friends ever missed a Friday night at The Club except for illness or death in the family. The decision was easy. In spite of the hour, she could barely wait to share the good news of her sales coup with her friends. The joy of it had spread from her heart to her lips, and she found herself smiling even though she was alone.

She locked the finished papers in her desk drawer and turned out the lights. The hallway seemed deserted and Sharon guessed that Bill must be in one of the other offices or on the second floor.

It was raining dead leaves. The beautiful fall colors had had their day, and those that were left were withered and dry. The early December wind was making short work of them, and they whipped by Sharon's face as she approached her car. The light jacket she had worn for her trip to Ohio wasn't enough. Time to bring out the heavy winter ones she mused as she reached into the depths of her purse for her keys.

The car was six years old and the miles she had put on it with this new job were aging it even faster. "I think your days are numbered, old friend," she informed it. The money she received for miles spent, plus the bonus she would get from this new account, all but cinched it. The Honda had served her well and she felt a pang at the thought of giving it up, but the thought of a new one helped.

The wind was howling with anger as it ungraciously grabbed the thin scarf she had stylishly wrapped around her neck and tossed it away. She reached for it as it flew upwards but there was nothing to do but watch it disappear

The Secret Monster Within

into the black night.

"Oh, no. One of my favorites," she wailed. How she hated wind. Snow, rain, sleet—she could accept any one of them, but the wind always struck terror in her heart. And tonight it seemed to be in one of its most violent moods.

The noise it generated covered all other sounds so she never heard his footsteps as he approached behind her. It wasn't until she felt his smooth hands surround her newly exposed neck that she realized she was not alone. And she knew, instinctively, that this unwelcome person was The Monster.

The hands were tightening and all the units of self-preservation that dwelled within her came to the fore. Her mind was so surprised at first, so dumbstruck that this could be happening to her, it all but failed her. But now the adrenaline flowed though her body and put her into the danger alert mode. She knew she had but a split second before she would be another victim of this serial killer.

She had to do something and quick as a flash she remembered reading that the elbow is the definitive weapon against an attack. She brought her hand up to her cheek and whipped her bent arm backward with all the fear-driven power she could muster. She felt her elbow hit the soft area of her attacker's stomach. "Omph." She heard his breath expel through his mouth that was but inches from her right ear. The hands on her neck loosened as he tried to catch his breath.

This was it, the only opportunity she would have to live through this horrible nightmare. She ran as fast as she could until the heel of her leather boot caught in the grate of a water drain. She fell on the cement and rolled over in time to see her tormentor just a few feet away. He had a brimmed hat pulled low over his forehead and a scarf wrapped around the lower part of his face so all she could see were his eyes, and they spit hate and murder with such venom, she could almost taste it.

She looked around for anything that might save her and found only a long, flexible branch that the wind had robbed from the willow tree. What good would this do? It would do nothing against this maniac whose intent was to kill her, but it was all she had and she whipped it at his face.

"You bitch!" he shouted. He put his hand up to his cheek where a bloody slash of the scarf revealed she had hit her mark.

"Hey. What's going on out there?" Bill had brought the trash out to the large containers located in the parking lot behind the office building. The wind whipped his voice away, but there was enough left that both Sharon and her attacker heard. The man attacking Sharon turned and looked at Bill.

"Help!" Sharon shouted at the top of her lungs. "Bill, help!"

Bill was in his forties but still retained the football physique he had been so proud of in his high school days. He dropped the trash bag and started to run to his fallen friend and the fiend who had done this to her.

The aggressor immediately decided this was not the time to put up a fight and instead ran to the side street where he disappeared into the blackness. Bill was torn with the choice of chasing Sharon's attacker or staying to see if she was all right, though it was quite simple, really. His practical mind acknowledged that he had no weapon and the attacker more than likely did, so why should he put his life on the line for what might result in nothing other than his own death? Instead he bent over Sharon and asked her how she was.

"Oh, Bill," she said through a torrent of tears. "You

The Secret Monster Within

saved my life. That was The Monster. I know it was. He tried to strangle me." Bill lifted her up and held her tight to his chest.

"Oh, my God. The Monster?" He shivered and it wasn't from the wind.

Chapter 24

"I wonder if The Monster realizes we have his DNA." Bernie raised his fist in a sign of victory. "Good God, Dan, we've got his DNA!" The Chief of Police was uncharacteristically exuberant.

They had a willow branch with The Monster's blood upon it, and a living, breathing victim/witness. It was their first real break. Granted, the victim, Sharon Kelly, couldn't provide much in the description field, but anything she could offer was helpful in their search for this maniac.

She had seen his eyes and they were brown. And the tone of the skin around them was that of a deep bronze. That eliminated all the blue-eyed blondes, so that alone took care of an enormous amount of the male population. He had been fairly tall, she recounted, but then, almost

The Secret Monster Within

anyone was tall compared to Sharon who was just a speck over the five-foot mark. But that did put all the really short ones in the not-interested file.

Bernie and Dan were right there with encouraging words. "Anything, anything at all that you can recall will be of tremendous help to us," they told the still-shaken victim.

Sharon told them that he only said two words, but it was enough so that she knew there was nothing remarkable about his voice, and there was no trace of an accent. Both Dan and Bernie conceded an accent would have helped, but you take what you can get.

Any tidbit of data was more than they had before, and so this was a geyser of info, since they were starting at zero. Bill Walkerman had been too far from the attacker to give any real descriptive details, but Sharon continued to tell the police all she could remember. She told them that he wore a light tan zippered jacket, and she was almost sure his trousers were a deep brown. The scarf around his neck and lower face was tan just like his jacket. "Imagine that," she had told the police, "a monster with a good sense of color coordination." She had tried to laugh, but the tears stung too much.

The blood on the willow branch was being tested against all known criminals who had an MO of murder with no rape and that, again, narrowed the field considerably. Sadly, there had been no matches so far, but they weren't done yet, so there was still hope.

***

Everyone looks for that one moment of fame that we've each been promised, and Sharon was no exception. Now she mocked it since this was nothing at all like she had envisioned it. However, if the truth were told, it wasn't a fair test since this wasn't really fame she was experiencing, it was notoriety. Her face had been splashed across the Saturday and Sunday editions of The Buffalo News and she had been the lead story on all three of the major local newscasts.

A MONSTER'S VICTIM LIVES TO TELL ABOUT IT! That, and words to that effect, were pretty much the lead-ins for all the stories. It was revealed that Sharon Kelly had looked into The Monster's eyes, and they were brown, and the skin surrounding these orbs of terror was of a bronze tone.

One of the reporters had dared to challenge these facts with a suggestion that The Monster could have been wearing brown-colored contact lenses and dark make-up to hide a fair complexion. But the police would later confirm that there was no trace of make-up on the willow branch that had cut his face, so the bronze tone was real enough, and that suggested that the brown eyes were too. The victim had further confirmed that The Monster was fairly tall but she wasn't sure of his exact height.

And Bill Walkerman had not been forgotten. He received all the hero's credit he was due.

***

It was Monday. Was it only three days ago that Sharon could barely wait for this day? Now that seemed like a lifetime ago and it almost was.

The new account she had been so proud of obtaining, the account that was to propel her to unexpected heights up the corporate ladder had received all the praise she had hoped for, but now it had lost its sparkle. Instead of being universally toasted as a star salesman, here she was, sequestered in her office with a policeman guarding her door.

The Secret Monster Within

She seethed with rage and knew that if she had a pistol and the opportunity to use it, she wouldn't think twice about killing her attacker. She hated him and what he had done to her with a sensation so strong she could almost taste its vile flavor. And what would that make her? There was only one answer.

Sharon had survived but she wasn't the same woman she had been before. To meet violent death face to face and survive was an experience few others could fathom. And her attacker was still out there. She had roused his anger because he had failed for the very first time, and she knew that in all probability that she was now his prime victim. How could she ever feel safe again until he was caught?

And the chances of that happening were remote to say the least. Twelve murders seven years ago, now so many again, and he was still out there, free as a bird. Up till now, the police had been almost clueless, and if the blood sample they got from the willow branch didn't identify The Monster soon, she knew her life was in imminent danger.

Suddenly the big account, the new car, the promotions all meant nothing. The Monster hadn't taken her life, but he had stolen what was good about it.

***

Bernie Roper had ordered around-the-clock police protection for his star witness, but it wasn't enough. He could have ordered the whole damn police force to sleep in her bedroom, and she still wouldn't feel safe.

"I want to move. I want to move to the other side of the world. Anywhere but here." Sharon's hard core had melted and she was a basket case of worry.

"I know how you must feel," Bernie told her in as soothing a tone as he could muster.

"You have no idea of how I feel!" she screamed at him.

"I can get you a permit for a pistol," he offered.

There it was, her opportunity. Wouldn't she just love to waste the life of the man who seemed to be wasting hers?

"A pistol?" she scoffed. "I've never held a gun in my life. I wouldn't know what to do with it."

"We'll teach you. I promise you will be the safest citizen in the Buffalo area."

"And if your promise fails, where will I be to hear your apology? Have you thought of that? Or don't you give a damn?"

Bernie knew it was fear talking. "I can't begin to tell you how much I care about getting this scumbag."

"And I'm your best chance, aren't I?" Sharon suddenly saw it all. She would be the catnip used to lure the cat. "Good God, I'm in more danger than I thought."

"No, no. Nothing like that." Bernie wasn't about to acknowledge that this thought had occurred to him. It was just too cold-blooded, and that wasn't Bernie. What is this monster doing to us all, he wondered?

***

Sharon got through the disappointing Monday. Oddly enough, Richard had retreated from the lecherous middle-aged man she knew only too well to that of a father figure. He gathered her into his arms and held her tightly. "Sharon, what a frightening experience you've had. I'm so sorry." And he sounded like he meant it.

He stood back and held her at arm's length. "You did a wonderful job obtaining that account in Cleveland. You broke all records, you know." He forced a smile as he shook his head in admiration.

The accolades were there and as good as she had hoped

The Secret Monster Within

they would be, but now they fell flat.

***

It was Tuesday and Sharon had just finished the paper work needed to set up the new account. She waved to the policeman guarding her office door. "Hey, Karl, I'm just going down to get some coffee? Want any?"

Karl Platt smiled at her friendly invitation. "Thanks, but I'm fine. Should I go with you?"

"You can't follow me around like a puppy dog." She smiled at the picture that painted. "Just watch my office so I'm sure The Monster won't be in there when I return. I'm just going to the cafeteria and I'll be right back. OK?"

"OK, Miss Kelly."

"Please. Call me Sharon."

"You've got it, Sharon."

He was so nice. She hated to think of the trouble she was about to cause him, but there was no other way.

Her co-workers stared at her as she walked through the central office. She was a newsworthy personality, but no one would have traded places with her. What a terrible cloud of fear she must be living under.

She smiled at them as bravely as she could.

Sharon opened the supply room door that led to a grassy knoll behind her office building. The door was locked from the inside and had no outside knob so Chief Roper had decided not to waste the limited police force he was allowed to cover a door that The Monster couldn't get into even if he tried. Sharon knew this, and hastily left her office building to cross a narrow open mall and an equally shallow treed area. She was now on the street that ran behind her office building, and looking right and left, she found it deserted except for one lonely car that crept slowly up to the point where she was standing.

"Hi, Sandy." She entered the passenger side of the car as quickly as possible, again looking in all directions to make sure no one saw her. "Let's go," she instructed her friend.

Sandy stepped on the gas but was careful not to exceed the speed limit. They definitely didn't want to call attention to themselves.

"The plane leaves at eleven. I should be able to make that," Sharon said while examining her watch. "Hopefully I'll be long gone before they think to check the airport."

She turned to her friend. "Sandy, I can't thank you enough for doing this for me. I want to be with my folks and away from this mad house. I'm so scared."

Sandy reached over to pat her friend's hand. "I know you are. I just hope you're doing the right thing, Sharon. But even if you aren't, I can understand why you want to get away from here." She shook her head "I know I'd want to run if I were you."

Sharon managed a weak smile. "Thanks. I'm giving up a lot, you know." Sandy knew all about Sharon's bonanza at work.

"You're not even telling them at Acme? You're just disappearing?"

"I'll call them from Florida. They'll understand that I need some time off." Sharon closed her eyes in a symbol of prayer. "At least I hope they do."

"Me too." Sandy saw the alarm in Sharon's eyes. "Oh, I'm sure they will."

"Here's the keys to my car, Sandy. When the police have left my apartment after they realize I'm gone, you can park it in my garage. I won't need it in Florida. Mom says I

The Secret Monster Within

can use her car for as long as I need it.

"And how long is that going to be?"

"Even I don't know that." Sharon threw her hands up. "Just pray they get this creep before I come back."

***

Bernie Roper couldn't believe it when he heard that Sharon had slipped away. He knew where she would be going. But then, so might The Monster.

Chapter 25

What was that? Jen was elated. It was but a little butterfly touch, but she knew it was the baby moving within her and she was filled with the wonder of it all.

"A little human being is growing inside of me." She would say this with so much awe that even those who had birthed many children would relive the miracle aspect of it.

Vince put his hand over her fast-growing abdomen, but could feel nothing. "It's too early. You'll feel it when the baby gets bigger," she assured her husband.

Since they had both decided they wanted to be surprised at the birth, they had planned no tests to determine the sex of the child. "We know it's an old cliché," they told everyone, "but we really don't care what it is. Just let it be

The Secret Monster Within

healthy." And so the baby would be addressed as It until the day it was born.

"At least we know the baby's alive and well. The doctor says so." Vince hugged her to him and kissed the top of her head. "But you're so tiny. How are you going to grow another human being inside that little body of yours?"

"Don't ask me, but little people have been doing it for as long as we've been blessed to be a part of this earth. I'm sure I'll be fine." Jen raised on her tiptoes to kiss her husband.

***

There had been much discussion as to where they would live after they were married. Of course, they had the option of staying in Vince's two-room apartment, but both had concurred that it was too small and it wasn't located in the best section of town, so that was scratched immediately.

But that left them with another dilemma. Jen's parents had been begging them to come live in their home, and they used all the powers of persuasion they could muster to sell that option to Jen and Vince.

"You'll use your old bedroom and have the run of the house. You'll have free room and board, and that's a real plus since Vince's main goal in the next six months is to finish and graduate from college." Vanessa's arguments made sense. They both knew that Vince would have to lessen his workload to get passing grades and that, of course, would result in less income.

The other choice was to use Jen's current housing—a bedroom with full run of a rented house. This would be costly since they would have to pay rent and food costs, but there was the distinct advantage of living close to Jen's employment, and since Vince would need his car to get to school, this was a large item.

What to do? Live inexpensively at her parents' house or have it more convenient to get to her job? They went back and forth until Jen shed tears of frustration.

"Come here, hon." Vince opened his arms to her. "Whatever you say is OK with me. It's just for a little while until I graduate and get a job. Whatever you want." He hugged her and gave an extra squeeze.

"I don't know," Jen wailed. "I'm torn."

"Let's go over the options one more time," Vince suggested.

"OK. You start." Jen was ready to throw in the towel.

Vince took a deep breath and searched for a beginning.

"We know if we stay where you are now, it will be costly because of the monthly rent and our food expenses. All that money could be saved if we stayed at your parents' house, and we could use it towards your getting a car. It wouldn't be a new one, but within a year you could get a decent one, and we both know how important that would be."

Jen nodded her head in visual agreement.

"So going to your parents' house sounds the best. But, and this is a big one, it would cost us our independence." Vince stared into her eyes to make sure she grasped the full meaning of this. "If we stay at your parents' house, you know they will be offering 'advice' all the time." Vince used his fingers to denote the quotes. "You will still be their little girl, and they will still be your parents. It goes with the territory. You know that, don't you?"

Jen said nothing, but again shook her head in agreement.

"Of course," Vince said, "it wouldn't be forever and we'd have that head start, so monetarily speaking, that would be a great help. But, then again, I know how much

The Secret Monster Within

you like Donna and Rob, and your independence, so here we go again."

"Oh, Vince. I feel like I'm on a seesaw. Or is it a merry-go-round? We're right back to where we started." Jen pressed her lips into a tight line.

"Well, hon, we both know what the smart thing to do is. There's no denying that staying with your folks will give us a head start. The question is, is it worth it? Giving up our independence, I mean." Vince looked at Jen with a shrug that pretty much tossed the problem right back in her lap.

"You're right, Vince. I love living here at Donna's and Rob's. It's so…so…" Jen searched for the word, "liberating."

"Look at your face when you said that." Vince cupped her chin in his hand. "That settles it. We will stay here at Donna's and Rob's, and if it gets to be too much, we'll always have the option of moving in with your folks. Right?"

"Oh, Vince. Yes! I think that's the right choice. I feel so much relieved, that it must be the right one." Jen raised her eyebrows, seeking confirmation.

"That's it, then. It's set in stone. We'll stay here with the option of moving in with your folks if it gets to be too much." Vince's eyes scanned the large rose-colored bedroom Jen was renting from the Mitchells. "At least we'll start off that way and see what happens."

Both Jen and Vince breathed a sigh of relief at the same time.

***

He watched her belly grow, day by day, week by week, and knew what he had to do. In spite of all his pleas, The Monster was adamant about it. It must be done, and done soon.

Chapter 26

It was fast approaching Christmas and Sharon was still visiting her folks in Florida. They had welcomed her with open arms, and she felt warm and safe for the first time since The Monster had attacked her. Acme had been most understanding although Richard was the only one in the office who knew where she was, and he still feared for her life. What if The Monster found out where she was staying and she had no police protection there?

Bernie Roper had assured Richard that the Orlando Police Department had been notified and was aware of the danger she was in. Unbeknownst to her or her family, there would be a plainclothesman assigned to watch her every move. Sharon never noticed the car with the blackened windows parked down the street from her parents' house.

The Secret Monster Within

***

The bitch must be on vacation. He guessed she was with her parents in Orlando. Maybe I should check it out and pay her a visit. Wouldn't that be a surprise? If not, she'll get hers when she gets home.
"Merry Christmas and Happy New Year, Sharon." Oh, no, wait. Maybe there won't be a New Year for you. Merry Christmas, you bitch. Hope it's a good one because it will be your last one. He couldn't resist a sardonic chuckle.

***

Vince had a secret he didn't want to share just yet, but how was he to go about it? He stared at the Sunday paper, and it was providence. Here was the perfect way.

"Jen. Look." He handed the paper to her.

"What?"

"Look at that airfare to Orlando, Florida. One hundred dollars round trip! Can you believe that?" Vince opened his eyes wide in a show of amazement.

"Yeah. So what?"

"So what? Hey, a day at Disneyland and a couple of days at the beach. So what? We can get there for a total of two hundred dollars!"

"Vince. We're trying to save money. We can't afford Disneyland right now. You know that."

"Well," Vince grudgingly conceded, "I guess you have a point. But for two-hundred dollars we can have a mini-vacation in the deep warm south." He emphasized and dragged out the *warm*. "Come on. This will be our one and only vacation till long after the baby's born. Please?"

"Vince," she reminded him once again, "we're trying to save money. A trip to Orlando is very extravagant, isn't it?"

"Not very. Just a little."

Jen knew of the amount of time Vince had been investing in his studies in order to graduate, and was also aware that he had been putting in too many hours at work, in spite of her frequent complaints. Deep in her heart, she knew he deserved this much.

"OK," she said, "but we have to be home for Christmas day. Right?"

"I wouldn't have it any other way." He smiled and gathered her into his arms.

To heck with the money, Jen said to herself. Sometimes you just have to do something to please yourself. So what if they would have to wait a month or two longer for her to get her car? The sun warmed her cold-from-the-north body in ways nothing else could. As she spread her arms to gather more rays, she was glad now that she had given in and agreed to this trip.

Vince had been so grateful that he couldn't have been nicer or more fun. It was turning out to be one of the best vacations she had ever had. That's why Vince's request seemed so out of place. "You what?" she asked in disbelief.

"Just for a couple of hours, honey. I won't be gone long. Promise."

"Why can't you tell me where you're going?"

"It's a surprise. I promise you it will be worth it."

Jen pouted, but gave in. Lying on the beach would be more fun with Vince at her side, but he promised he would be gone for only a couple of hours and further promised that she would be pleasantly surprised. So, why not?

"OK," she granted, but she made sure he heard her sigh of discontent.

It was closer to three hours before Vince returned. He

The Secret Monster Within

hoped she wouldn't think to ask how much the taxi cost him.

"Where have you been?" she demanded.

His downcast face didn't promise as pleasant a response as he had predicted. Instead, he closed his eyes and grimaced. "I'm sorry, honey. I thought I was going to come back with some fantastic news." He shrugged his shoulders in a form of defeat. "But I'm not."

Jen's continued stare demanded more of an explanation then that.

"I saw an ad in the employment section of The Buffalo News for a job here in Orlando. When I saw the low airfare and you agreed to come here with me, I thought I'd apply for it in person. It was fantastic pay and it came with a company car. You could have had mine then." He was talking so fast, she could barely keep up with him.

His enthusiasm waned as he continued. "Well, as you can guess, I didn't get it. 'You're too young. You're not even out of school yet! We need someone with experience.' He mimicked his prospective employer's voice. "Darn it," he added in his own.

"Vince. You were thinking of applying for a job all the way down here in Florida? Without even consulting me?" Jen looked at him like he was a complete stranger.

"I thought you'd be thrilled. It offered great pay and had lots of fringe benefits." What's wrong with women, Vince wondered?

"Well, you were wrong!" Jen's pleasant mood from the past two days dissipated into thin air. "Something this drastic is something we would have to discuss together. This isn't a one-man team, you know."

"I never said it was. This was just," he spluttered as he searched for the right words, "just something I thought you'd be thrilled about. It was like a surprise gift I was going to give you. Can't you see that?"

"Well," Jen's mouth widened into a conciliatory grin, "I guess your heart was in the right place. Even if your brain wasn't!" she couldn't resist adding.

Jen put her arms around Vince's waist and laid her head on his chest. "At least we got a beautiful three-day vacation out of it. I thank you for that!"

"Oh, honey, I love you so much." Vince leaned over and kissed her with so much intensity, it almost took her breath away.

Chapter 27

It was a picture perfect Christmas. Buffalo winters are notorious and most outsiders would guess that a white Christmas was a certainty, but they would be wrong. There have been some warm slushy ones, and even some green ones, but this year it looked like a winter scene from the front of a Christmas card.

The deep blue sky served as a backdrop for the snow-trimmed trees, and the sun transformed the landscape into a wonderland of sparkling jewels. Jen and Vince admitted that although they missed the warmth of Florida, neither could imagine living a year without enjoying a day like today. And who needed the tropic warmth when you had family to greet you with open arms?

"Merry Christmas!" Jen's parents opened the door and

their hearts to their only child and her husband.

"And Merry Christmas to you," both Jen and Vince answered at once. Their voices were accompanied with a mist of frothy white breath.

"Oh, I smell the turkey. Ummm." Jen closed her eyes and took a deep breath to savor it all the more.

"We got a nice one this year. Hope it tastes as good as it looks." Vanessa took her daughter's coat.

"No one need to guess whether you're pregnant or not." Vanessa patted her daughter's tummy. " That baby's growing by the minute." She smiled at her daughter.

"It sure is," Jen acknowledged. "I can feel it moving inside me now."

"Oh, honey. This is so exciting, and I'm so happy for you." Vanessa kissed her daughter's cold lips. "And how's Daddy doing?" Vanessa asked as she turned to her son-in-law.

"Just fine. Thanks, Mom." Vince kissed his mother-in-law on the cheek, and then handed his coat to Troy.

"Welcome home," Troy said, as he shook Vince's hand. "How was the vacation?"

"Too short," Vince said.

Troy chuckled. "What did you do?"

"Well, Disneyland's outside our budget, so we just laid on the beach and soaked up the sun. Big belly and all!" Jen added with a laugh.

"Oh. Except for a few hours. Tell my folks what you did last Thursday, Vince."

Vince looked startled. He didn't think Jen would bring this up in front of her parents. "Well, I, ah, I, um…"

"You didn't rob a bank, did you?" Troy was laughing at Vince's struggle.

"Not really. But something almost as bad, at least as far as Jen is concerned." Vince looked at Jen who was shaking

The Secret Monster Within

her head in agreement.

Vince raised his eyes in a you-can't-win gesture and continued. "I really thought I was doing something special. I had seen a job advertised in The News that offered great pay and a company car, everything we would need to get a good start as soon as I'm out of school. I was saving it as a surprise. But," Vince wobbled his head side to side, "looks like I'm the one who got the surprise."

"What do you mean?" Troy asked.

"They said I was too young and too inexperienced for the job. They lost interest the minute they learned that I wasn't even out of college yet."

"Well, that's too bad, Vince. But I'm sure you'll find another one real soon. Why were you so upset, honey?" Vanessa turned to her daughter.

"Mom. The job was in Orlando, Florida! You wouldn't get to see us very often, and that includes this little one too." She patted her stomach.

"In Florida? Oh." Vanessa looked stricken. "I'm sorry, Vince, but I'm glad you didn't get it." Vanessa could see she was hurting her son-in-law, but what the heck. He almost stole her family from her. She just couldn't imagine that happening, especially now when she had a grandchild on the way.

"I'm a very practical fellow, Vince, but I must side with my wife and daughter on this one." Troy's furrowed brow told how he felt. "You'll find a job up here, son. Don't be looking for one that's thousands of miles away. Please."

Vince grinned and nodded his head. "You got it, Dad." He reached to shake Troy's hand as a sign of agreement, but Troy pulled him up and gave him a hug.

"Family. That's more important than anything else, Vince. Don't ever forget that."

Chapter 28

Bernie Roper had spent the Christmas holiday with Dan, although Drew wasn't with him this time. The two of them had bached it, and each was grateful for the other's company.

In spite of the Christmas music, sparkling lights, and the general feeling of good will that permeated the air during this holiday season, they couldn't help but talk about the one thing neither of them could get out of their minds-- The Monster.

"He must be taking time off for the Christmas holidays. Of course, he's probably lying low now that someone has seen him." Dan shrugged his shoulders as he was forced to admit that as good as that sounded, Sharon had only seen his eyes.

The Secret Monster Within

"That could very well be, but you have to admit, it's more than we've had all these years totaled." Bernie looked to Dan for some encouraging words.

"Yeah. You're right on that score." Dan could sense Bernie's hunger for anything that might lift his spirits, and it was the holiday season of good cheer. Who was he to pour water on the little fire Bernie had kindled?

"I've been in touch with Chief Walker in Orlando. All's quiet at the Kelly house, but I suspect Sharon will be returning to Buffalo soon after the holidays. We'll have to keep an eye out for her."

"That's for sure," Dan agreed. "The Monster might just be biding his time till she gets back. He must know by now that she isn't here, and I just hope to hell he hasn't figured out where she is."

"Me too," Bernie emphasized. "But like I said, I've been in touch with Chief Walker ever since she left. He's been keeping me up-to-date and I don't think we have to worry until Sharon comes home again. That is, *if* she comes home again. I don't know if I would if I were her."

"Well, the same thought occurred to me," Dan said. "I wonder what The Monster would do if she didn't return."

"Who knows what goes on in that warped mind of his?"

***

Sharon's sad eyes told it all. "I hate leaving here," she said. "I've had such a wonderful Christmas."

"Oh, honey, you were the best gift of all. We'll miss you so much." Her mother reached to give her a hug. "Please don't go, Shar. Please," she begged once more.

"I have to, Mom, but thanks. I'll be careful. I promise."

"I'm so worried for you." Her mother caressed her cheek.

"I have police protection and lots of locks on my door.

I'll be fine." Sharon wished she felt as confident as she sounded.

"Call us as soon as you get home," her father told her for what seemed like the millionth time. "Don't forget."

"I will. I promise." Sharon kissed her parents once more and reluctantly left them to go to Gate 7 from which her plane was leaving. She turned for a last-minute wave and hoped they couldn't see the tears in her eyes.

She had felt safe here amidst the warmth of her family's love. Now she was returning to a lonely apartment and a job she no longer cared about, at least not like she used to. And worse yet, she was returning to a place where a monster had tried to kill her once, and may be planning a second attack. But in spite of her parents' pleas for her to remain with them in Florida, she had remained adamant. Her life was in Buffalo, and this maniac wasn't about to ruin it, not if she had anything to say about it.

Except for one brief moment when she had looked into the eyes of a stranger who was walking by her parents' house, she had felt safe. There was something about his eyes that reminded her so much of The Monster's, it gave her chills. She realized the foolishness of her fear. She was miles away from his lair. He wouldn't be here. Would he?

"No," she had actually said out loud. She scoffed at her irrational fear and returned to her parents' house with the mail. And then she had erased the chance meeting with a stranger from her mind and dismissed it as inconsequential.

But now Christmas was over, and she had a life to return to.

***

Richard seemed rather aloof. He hadn't offered the warm reception Sharon had been counting on.

The Secret Monster Within

"Hi, Sharon," he said, and gave her a little hug around the shoulders. "How are you doing?"

"Well, I'm usually happy to return home after a vacation, but...," her voice trailed off as she search for the right words to describe her feelings.

"I can well imagine. It's been a rough time for you, I'm sure." Richard's business-like tone alerted Sharon to trouble brewing.

He had asked her to come into his office the moment she arrived, and she now sat on the opposite side of his desk. Richard walked back to his chair and pressed his fingertips together.

"Sharon," he paused, obviously seeking the right words, "we at Acme know you obtained one of the biggest accounts this company's ever had. Don't think we don't appreciate it." He leaned forward, and said, "Believe me when I say that."

All of her defenses went up, and she knew she was going to hear some bad news. She took a deep breath and closed her eyes. "But what?" she asked.

"But," Richard acknowledged with a tip of his head, "you've been gone for some time now and someone had to take over your account. We gave it to Tommy."

He saw the surprise and anger in her eyes. "Hey, what could we do, Sharon? You weren't here, were you?"

"Well, no, but..."

Sharon shook her head. "Richard," she conceded, "you couldn't do anything else. I know that." Tears sparkled in the tough gal's eyes. "But when I think of what this monster has stolen from me, it makes me sick."

Richard rose from his seat and came over to her chair. "Come here, hon," he said and he took her hand and raised her so she was standing in front of him. "Talk to Tommy," he suggested. "I think the two of you can work something out with this account."

"Yeah. I'm sure," Sharon said sarcastically, as she turned to leave.

***

Tommy was on the road so she had the office to herself. She had always liked the glass partitions as they provided some semblance of quietness while still enabling her to see her fellow employees. She smiled and waved to them, but this time it didn't give her the feeling of comfort and camaraderie she used to feel. And at five o'clock, everyone was only too happy to leave their place of business to go to their safe and secure home.   Everyone but Sharon.

In spite of the bitter news regarding her account, she didn't want to leave the office to go to her empty apartment. In fact, she dreaded it. Even with the police protection, she didn't feel safe there, at least not as safe as she did here at the heavily populated office. She was almost the last to leave although she made sure there were still some people ahead of her and in the parking lot when she went to her car. No more would she venture out there alone. Never again!

She drove to her apartment and could see no sign of the police protection she had been promised, but she knew it was there. Hopefully, if she couldn't see it, neither could he. She unlocked her door with shaking hands and entered her apartment.

It was beautifully appointed. She had, at one time, thought of becoming an interior decorator since she had such a flare for it. Why waste all that talent, her friends had told her? Get paid for it. And she would have loved doing it too. But like most of life, you reach a fork in the road and make a choice, and then you have to live with what you chose.

The Secret Monster Within

Not that she wasn't happy with what she was doing. Being in sales suited her outgoing personality and she was good at it. Damn good. But, she mused as her eyes swept the lovely apartment, I would have done pretty well at decorating too.

The soft beige, burgundy and gold with splashes of deep olive green offered a serene and elegant vista. Then she turned to close the many locks she had installed on her door, the only jarring discord.

Look what you've done, you fiend. You've ruined my life and my décor.

***

Sharon didn't know how she could face Tommy when he returned from Ohio. He had been working on *her* account. Pfft. Better just eat it. It's Tommy's account now. He didn't have to do anything to get it except not be a victim of The Monster. They always go after the weaker sex. Why do women have to pay such a price for not being born with the muscle power that men have? It just isn't fair. If it hadn't been for Bill and his muscle power, she would have been one more victim added to the ever-growing list of The Monster's dead. God, why couldn't you give us muscles too?

She was still frowning as she thought of the injustice of it all when the office door opened and Tommy appeared. No matter how many times she saw him, she was still amazed by his good looks. He could wear anything off the rack and make it look good. He was tall, sported broad shoulders and narrow hips and had extremely long legs. Oh, how she envied those long legs. His golden brown hair was brushed back in waves and was neatly trimmed, and his clean-shaven square jaw added to his manliness. And now his blue eyes sparkled, and he was all smiles.

Just what I need...a happy victor. Go ahead. Just cram it down my throat till I choke on it.

"Hello, Tommy," she managed to say.

"Hi, Sharon. Nice to have you back." The smile was brilliant, but then, why not?

He saw her face and adjusted his. "Hey, you've been through a rough ordeal. Really, how are you doing?" Tommy looked genuinely concerned.

Oh, sure, like you really care. "I'm doing OK, thanks."

"That's good. I can't imagine how horrible it must have been for you."

"No, you'd have to live through it yourself to know what it's like. And I hope you never do." She was surprised to realize she really meant that. For crying out loud, it wasn't his fault. Deep down, she knew that.

"Well, as you know, I just got back from Ohio. They all said to give you their best when I saw you."

"Thanks, Tommy. Nice of them to remember me." As soon as she said it, she realized how sarcastically flat it sounded. "I didn't mean for it to sound that way," she added quickly. "I'm sure they were genuinely concerned."

"Well, they were. Just as we all are. Is there anything I can do?"

Yeah. Like give me back my account. "No, thanks, Tommy. Just got to get back in the swing of things."

"Well, maybe this will be a good start," he said as he handed her the heavy folder he was carrying.

"What's this?" she asked as she placed it on her desk.

"Take a look and see," he said with a cockeyed grin.

Sharon's mouth opened in a state of wonder when she did so. It was her Ohio account, all up-to-date. "Tommy!"

"It's yours, Shar. I just kept it warm till you returned."

"What?" She was aghast and still staring at him.

The Secret Monster Within

"Hello," he said. "I don't rob other people's accounts. What I get, I'll get on my own. This one's yours, Sharon. You worked for it and you deserve it. That fiend did enough to you. He can't rob you of this too."

"Tommy," she said as she rose to embrace him. "I can't believe you're doing this."

"Why not? Who do you think I am?"

"Who do I think you are? Just about one of the nicest people I've been blessed to know. That's all."

"Thanks, Sharon. It took something like this to wake me up, but I think you are too. We're a team, right?"

"The best damn sales team in the whole US." Sharon laughed which was a rare occurrence of late, and held out her hand to shake on it.

So there, Monster. You didn't rob me of everything.

Chapter 29

"I can't believe you did that!" Vince's eyes flashed fire and a look of scorn turned his soft mouth into a grimace of distaste.

"What are you talking about?" Jen feigned an act of innocence. She knew what he was talking about, but she wasn't about to acknowledge it.

"Here. Give me your coat," he said harshly. They had just returned home from a holiday party at Marilyn and Charles Comanski's house.

Jen obediently removed the winter coat and handed it to her husband.

"You know darn well what I'm talking about. Don't act so innocent."

"Oh, for crying out loud, Vince." Jen rolled her eyes in

The Secret Monster Within

a what's-the-big-deal gesture. "It was only one glass of wine. One!" she emphasized with a raised finger.

"Hey. One glass of wine is the same as one beer or one shot of whiskey. You know you're not supposed to have any alcohol while pregnant. Not any!"

"Have I had one drink since I found out I was pregnant?" The fire was contagious and Jen shouted the accusation.

"No. None that I know of, and well you shouldn't."

"None that you know of? What does that mean?"

"I mean I've never seen you take a drink, at least not when I was around. Who knows what you do when I'm not here."

"What?"

"Let's face it, Jen. You like your drinks. I've seen that time and time again. It's hard to believe you've stopped just like that." Vince snapped his fingers and his scornful look multiplied the accusation.

The volume of their voices had increased and Jen knew that Donna, Rob and Gerri could hear their argument. She took a deep breath and tried to talk in a more normal voice.

"Vince. Calm down. I swear to you on a bible, on all I hold dear, that I've not had a drink since I learned I was pregnant until tonight." She raised her hand and shook her head. "I swear it!"

Vince stared at her, obviously weighing whether to believe her or not. His whole body sagged in a display of surrender. "OK. I'm sure you haven't. Come here, honey." He reached out for her.

The tears trickled down Jen's cheeks as she meekly went to her husband and laid her head against his chest.

He put his arms around her and pressed her to him. "I don't know why I said that. I shouldn't have. It's just seeing you drink that wine…well… I..." Vince gave up trying to find the right thing to say and instead kissed the top of her head.

"I know you're right," Jen whispered. "I shouldn't have had the wine. But everyone was drinking and having so much fun. I just wanted to be a part of it, just for one moment."

She raised her tear-stained face to her husband. "I won't do it again. I promise."

"Oh, honey, you know how much I love you. And I love this little being you're carrying inside of you. I just want to give him or her as good a chance as possible. You understand that, don't you?"

"Of course I do, Vin. And so do I. I don't think that one glass of wine is going to make much difference, but I swear to you, it will be last one I have till the baby is born."

"I believe you." Vince smiled and hugged her to him once more.

The shouting had stopped, and Donna and Rob relaxed, knowing the worst was over. Everyone has fights.

***

"Hi, Mr. and Mrs. Lopez." Jen smiled at her church-going friends.

"Hello, Jennifer. Vince. How nice to see you." Ken smiled at the young couple.

"How are you feeling, honey?" Maureen couldn't help but notice how far along Jen was in her pregnancy.

"I'm just fine, Mrs. Lopez. Thanks." Jen rolled her eyes. "Finally over that morning sickness. Ugh."

"I was lucky, I guess," Maureen offered. "Never had to

The Secret Monster Within

suffer with that with any of my pregnancies."

"Well, take it from one who knows...you *were* lucky. Not much fun," Jen offered with more rolling eyes.

"Kyle called and Rachel said to say hello to you and Mrs. Longfellow if I saw you," Maureen said. "She really likes you both, you know."

"Well, that makes us even then, 'cause we really like her too." Jen smiled as she remembered the Lopez's darling granddaughter.

"Where are your folks, Jen?" Ken looked around to find the missing parents.

"I thought they were right behind us. They must have run into some friends to talk with." Jen turned to look at the crowd that was exiting behind them. "Oh, here they come," she said.

Troy and Vanessa gave a welcoming smile as they squeezed through the crowded aisle. "Hi, Ken. Hi, Maureen." Troy offered his hand.

"Nice to see you," Ken said.

"Looks like your new grandbaby is doing fine," Maureen said with a smile.

"Isn't she getting big?" Vanessa put her arms around her daughter's shoulders and puffed with pride.

"She certainly is," Maureen agreed. "Getting uncomfortable?" she asked Jen.

"A little. But it still seems like such a miracle to me, I don't mind it a bit," Jen said as she rubbed her ever-growing stomach. "Well," she laughed, "maybe a little."

"That's one thing about being pregnant," Maureen said, "you get so enthralled over the thought of what is happening, you don't mind the little discomfort at the beginning. But let me assure you, Jen, by the time you are in your eighth or ninth month, you'll be counting the days to delivery. Believe me." Maureen nodded her head just in case Jen didn't get the message.

"So I've heard." Jen laughed. "I can't wait to meet this little one."

"Nor can we," said her mother.

Chapter 30

What was that? Maureen stopped making the bed and walked to the shaded window so she might hear better. She heard it again, and it sounded like Ken calling from outside. Well, for heaven's sake, why can't he open the front door and talk to me? I'm supposed to drop everything and run down the stairs just because he doesn't want to take the time or trouble to open the door. I've a good mind to ignore him. Noble idea, of course, but not one she would follow through on. Maureen sighed in exasperation, and then walked down the stairs.

"What do you want, Ken?" she asked none too politely as she opened the door. A blast of freezing cold wind took her breath away as she did so.

"Ken!" she shouted when she saw her husband lying on

the walk leading from their front porch. "What happened?" Ignoring the cold, she ran outside with nothing but a light sweater to protect her from the elements.

"I slipped on black ice," he said. "I think I've broken my leg."

"Oh, my God. No!"

"Maureen, call 911. I can't get up."

"And you're bleeding," she told him.

"It's OK," he said. "It's just a little cut on my face. It's my leg that's bad."

"I'll be right back," she said as she ran back into the house.

There was nothing for Ken to do but lie there and wait for help. Maureen was back at his side within minutes. "They'll be right here," she assured him, as she dabbed at his bleeding cheek.

"Get Lady," he said. Lady was finally living up to her name as she sat by his side with the leash lying loose beside her.

"Can you believe it?" Ken shook his head in wonder. "She's free to run, but she knows I'm hurt, and she's staying right here, next to me." They both stared in wonder at their dog. This was so unlike Lady who would normally run them ragged any time she got loose, making it one of her favorite games as they tried to catch her. But this time she intuitively knew this wasn't a game, and she sat quietly by her injured master's side.

"What a good girl you are," Maureen told her. "Come here, sweetie." She grabbed the leash and led her dog into the house. "No walk today, I'm afraid." Lady wagged her tail and then turned and whined when Maureen left to go back to Ken.

"Maureen, get a coat on. You'll catch your death of pneumonia." Ken might be down but he was still in charge.

The Secret Monster Within

It had been such a shocking event that Maureen hadn't realized how cold she was. "Yeah, you're right. I'll be right back," she told him over her shoulder as she scrambled through the front door, being careful not to let Lady out.

It was but a minute later that she returned with a coat and gloves and scarf. She was still buttoning the coat as she stepped on the front porch. "That feels better," she admitted.

They could hear Lady's pleading cries through the closed door.

"Be a good girl," she shouted to her dog.

"She's worried about you," she said as she turned back to her husband.

"I know," Ken said. "She is a good girl."

They both heard the siren at the same time.

"There they are," Maureen said with great relief as the ambulance pulled up in front of their home.

Ken had to stay in the hospital for three days where they taught him how to get in and out of cars, go up and down the stairs, and even how to use a toilet. He couldn't believe how inconvenient it was or how totally clumsy he felt with a full-leg cast that went from his ankle to his hip, but luckily he had strong upper-body strength and he mastered the art of crutches quite easily.

The cut on his face was deeper than he thought and required a series of stitches, and it would leave a scar. "How about that," he teased his wife. "Matching scars. One on each side of my face now." He laughed as he pointed to the one he had gotten sometime earlier when he had been whipped by a tree branch while walking Lady. "Damn dog." He laughed again. Maureen cocked her head and looked up in a gesture that pretty much said it all.

Troy, Vanessa, Jen and Vince stopped by after church

every Sunday to drop off a few fun things like word puzzles, reading material, hand lotion, etc. They were happy to check in with their dear friend, and it wasn't wasted either. Ken was touched that they cared enough to do that.

***

There were no murders over the holidays and Bernie and Dan accepted that as an extra Christmas present. It's tough enough to lose a loved one anytime, but over the holidays? Zing, right to the heart.

But now the holidays were over and the long bleak winter months of January, February and March loomed ahead. They both knew what was coming but there was nothing either one could do except sit and take it on the chin, and look more and more inept.

***

"Where is he? And what the hell is he doing?" Dan verbalized the questions everyone was thinking.

"Damned if I know." Bernie shook his head. "Bad weather never stopped him before."

"Well, let's hope he hasn't turned into a fair-weather murderer. Tomorrow's April Fools Day, and I wouldn't put it past him. He likes nothing better than to make fools of us. What a perfect day for a murder." Dan threw up his hands.

"Jeez. I never thought of that," Bernie said. "And I hope The Monster doesn't either!" he added.

Chapter 31

Jen waddled into Playground For Kids and took off the coat she could no longer button. She was fast learning that all the late pregnancy inconveniences the experienced mothers had warned her about at the beginning of her pregnancy were indeed coming true. Just getting in and out of a chair was quite the chore, and walking, which was one of her favorite pastimes just a few months earlier, was now a challenge.

Still, she knew this was a small price to pay for these obvious signs that her baby was growing big and strong, and that made it all worthwhile. So what's a little backache compared to the ultimate reward she was about to know in just a little over two months?

The children at Playgounds had been noticing her growing girth, and she had been only too happy to tell them about the baby growing inside of her. She had even let them touch her stomach, and they all squealed when they felt the baby move.

Melanie Longfellow smiled at Jen. "Hi, Mommy. How are you doing?"

"Just fine, thanks." It was easy to return her smile.

"I'm going to miss you when you become a mother, you know." Melanie made a sad face as though she needed to confirm it.

"It'll only be for a little while," Jen said. "When this little one is six months old, I'll be bringing him or her to work with me." She rubbed her stomach once more. "You did say that was all right, didn't you?"

"It will be just fine, and no charge for this little playmate." Melanie laughed as she pointed to Jen's unborn child.

"Have I got the perfect job or haven't I? Thanks, Mrs. Longfellow."

"Jen, you know what?" Jen's employer nodded her head. "I think you've been here long enough now that it might be time you called me by my first name. Don't you?" Melanie Longfellow raised her brows in the form of a question.

Jen grimaced and made a face. "Gee, I don't know if I can do that. I've been calling you Mrs. Longfellow for such a long time. Like, ever since I've known you." Jen shrugged her shoulders and said, "But thanks for offering. I'll try."

"Only if you want to, Jen. Whatever you like." Mrs. Longfellow smiled at her young employee.

" OK…Melanie." Jen choked a little on the unfamiliar address.

Melanie Longfellow chuckled. "You'll get used to it.

The Secret Monster Within

Come here, hon." She gave Jen a peck on the cheek and told her once more how happy she was for her and her soon-to-be-born baby.

"You're going to be a mother, and you'll love it. I know I did."

"How many children do you have again?" Melanie had talked to Jen about her family over the past two years, but the total number had slipped her mind.

"Five." Melanie held up her hand with five splayed fingers.

"Wow. You sure had your hands full, didn't you?"

"Well, I guess I did. And I'm not going to lie to you, being a parent is hard work, and can be frustrating and very tiring. But," she smiled as she paused, "you get so many happy rewards in return." She chuckled and shook her head as she thought about some of them. "Just like anything, you'll have to live it to know it, and you'll know what I mean in the years to come."

"Of course," she continued, "mine are all grown now, and I have grandchildren and two great-grandchildren." Melanie shook her head in amazement. "It doesn't seem possible. Time goes by so fast."

Jen knew how old Melanie was but still found it hard to believe. No one in their late sixties should have skin that was as finely smooth and firm as hers, and she didn't hesitate to share her feelings.

"Why thank you, honey." Melanie beamed her appreciation.

Jen felt the friendly glow and thought this might be a good time to ask a question she had often wondered about, but thought too personal to ask.

"I know you were a widow... Melanie," she emphasized the first name salutation, "but how long has your first husband been gone now?"

"Oh, my. Let me think." Melanie closed her eyes and added up the years.

"Yes," she said with a nod. "It's been going on twenty years." She paused and shook her head. "Sometimes it seems just like yesterday."

And even after so long a time, Jen could see the tears welling in Melanie's eyes.

"He must have been fairly young then," Jen offered, hoping Melanie would give further information without being asked.

"Oh, yes, he was. Barely fifty years old." Melanie closed her eyes, and Jen could see the pain on her face.

Oh, no. What have I done? Jen realized she shouldn't have brought the subject up. It's none of my business. When will I learn, she admonished herself? She couldn't think of a thing to say to Melanie that would ease the pain.

"I was driving, you know. That's what makes it even more difficult for me, even though I know it wasn't my fault." Melanie's eyes were open wide as she relived that tragic day one more time.

"Oh, it was a car accident?" Darn it. Shut up, Jen. Leave it alone.

"Yes, it was. And I thank God every day that the kids were grown and off on their own. It was just Ron and I in the car. We were coming from a vacation in Pennsylvania and we were almost home!" She said this as though it really made a difference.

"It was a bright sunlit day, and we were climbing that big hill down in South Wales. I was almost to the crest of the hill when a car appeared right in front of us, on our side of the road. There was nothing I could do.

Jen gasped as the picture became clear.

"It seems a teenager didn't have the patience that an older and wiser driver would have had to wait for the slow-

The Secret Monster Within

moving truck that was in front of him on a steep hill." A tear trickled down Melanie's cheek.

"I had a broken leg and arm and some cracked ribs, but I survived." She closed her eyes once more and shook her head in bewilderment. "I have no idea how or why I lived, and Ron didn't. Nor did the teenager."

Jen reached over to touch Melanie's hand. "I'm so sorry," she said with conviction.

"Thank you, honey." Melanie smiled at the caring words of this young girl, and then took a deep breath before continuing.

"Ron left me with five beautiful children, and also a house that was paid for, a healthy investment portfolio, and a sizeable insurance policy. I was OK, monetarily speaking, but I was alone. It took some time to get over the shock of his being gone. This man that I had lived with for almost thirty years, this man whom I had shared all my joys and sorrow with, this man who helped me bring up a family, this man...." Melanie paused to wipe a tear. "It wasn't easy, Jen."

She looked up and saw Jen's eyes were misting as well. "Oh, honey. I shouldn't be burdening you with all this sorrow. I'm sorry." Melanie sat up straight and put on as happy a face as possible.

"I lived like that for almost ten years," Melanie continued, "filling my time with baby-sitting grandchildren, getting involved in charity work, joining clubs, etc., etc." Melanie waved her hand at the banality of it all. "And then, ten years later, I met Jack Longfellow, a widower who, as you know, is now my husband. He knew that I needed more than this, and it was Jack that saw this business for sale in the Sunday paper."

"He encouraged me to look into it, and here I am, earning money and doing something I really enjoy doing. And bless his heart, Jack has retired from his electrical business, and he loves to cook. He always has my dinner waiting for me when I get home from here. I mean, could life be any better?" Melanie couldn't resist a little giggle.

"Well, the children at Playground for Kids are lucky to have you," Jen said. "And so am I." Jen reached over to touch Melanie's hand, and there was a moment of bonding.

Their moment of camaraderie was broken by loud screams. Lexi and Amie were fighting over a doll, and Jen rushed to break up the spat.

"That's my doll," Lexi screamed.

"I had it first!" Amie was not to be denied.

Jen took charge. "Here, now," she said with great authority, "let me have the doll."

Lexi and Amie both screamed at the same time when Jen took their treasure away from them.

"Whoa. Wait. Look what I've got." Jen mentally crossed her fingers as she reached into a bag she had brought to work with her. "How do you like these?"

She revealed two large teddy bears she had bought at the dollar store.

"Ooo." The sobs subsided, as both little girls reached for the new toys at once.

Jen looked at Melanie and raised her eyes in a gesture of gratitude, and received a nod of approval in return.

Chapter 32

Vince put on a good front, but he was actually fearful over the prospect of becoming a father. He had finally, FINALLY, as his mother put it, graduated from college and was looking for employment. "God," he pleaded, "please let me find a job. I've got a baby coming and a bride who will soon be a new mother. Help me, please." He couldn't remember when he had prayed so hard before. He knew it took more than a prayer to get a job, but hey, any port in a storm. He looked around the rose-colored bedroom and longed for the day when they would have a job, a baby and a home of their own.

***

"Good morning, Vince." Jen smiled at her husband who had finally awakened. He managed to open one eye.

"Is it morning already?" He laughed.

"Well, it won't be for long. Better get up and at 'em." She pulled the covers off her sleepy spouse.

"Hey. It's cold. Brrr. Come here, wench. Keep me warm."

"Vin, I'm all dressed. I've been up for over an hour."

"So?"

"So I'm not dressed for bed anymore."

"Who cares? Come here." He patted the empty space next to him. "It's lonely here," he said with a tragic face. "Come keep me company," he pleaded.

"You're a nut," she said as she lay down beside him.

"Here. Let me fix that for you." Vince started to unbutton Jen's maternity top.

"Vin!"

"What?" He continued with the job at hand. "There," he said as he slid it off her shoulders.

"Now, just a little adjustment here." He reached behind her and undid her bra.

"Ooo. Look at those babies," he exclaimed as her full breasts escaped their snare. Jen couldn't resist a laugh.

He softly caressed one breast while he put his mouth to the other. Then he kissed both breasts.

"Don't want to show any favoritism," he explained to her in all seriousness.

They both laughed at his silliness.

What a lucky baby you're going to have," he told her.

"I think I'm going to have two!" She laughed as she pointed to her stomach and then to Vince.

"Well, I won't mind sharing," he said. "Not much, anyway," he said with a lecherous look.

Saturdays were fun. No school, no church. Just a morn-

The Secret Monster Within

ing art class for Jen and then the whole day for themselves. They relished this day every week.

"Here," he said. "I don't want to ignore It." He put his hand under the elastic waist of her maternity slacks and rubbed her very swollen belly.

"By the way, have we thought of anything better than 'It' for a name yet?"

"Hey," she said, "*It* was good enough for the Adams Family." Jen laughed. "What's wrong with *It*?"

"Hmmm, maybe nothing. 'It' it will be. It Marotti. Has a nice ring to it, doesn't it? Whoops. Another 'it'. Any chance we might get mixed up with our its? How about…" Vince raised his eyes and pursed his lips in a show of great thought. "I know. How about tit?" He laughed as he grabbed both breasts with each of his hands. "And I've the perfect second name too. How about 'for tat'? There you go…Tit For Tat. OK? Agree?"

"Vin, you are a nut, and I love you." Jen gave him a quick kiss and then put her legs over the side of the bed. "But playtime is over. Now get up, you lazybones. You have an interview for a job," she said while pointing to her watch, "and I have an art class to attend."

"Slave master," he growled.

"Oh, Vin!" Jen looked stricken.

"What is it, hon?"

Jen ran from the room without a word.

"Jen!" Vince jumped out of bed and ran after her. "What's wrong?"

He arrived at the bathroom and the door was shut and locked.

"Jen!" he called through the closed door. "Let me in. What's wrong?"

"Wait." He heard her muffle a cry.

It was but a minute when she opened the door. She was

holding her panties, and the red stain told it all.

"I'm losing our baby."

"Oh, my God." He couldn't hide the panic he felt. "Tidy up, hon, while I call the doctor."

He kissed her on the cheek and pulled out his cell phone. "Do you have any pain?" he asked while dialing the doctor's number.

"No. None at all," she sobbed.

Vin had gotten a clean pair of panties and a protective pad for her while waiting for the phone to be answered. "Here," he said. "And don't get in a dither till we see what the doctor has to say. OK?"

"Easier said then done," she said, while putting on the clean underwear. "Oh, Vinnie. I'm losing our baby," she wailed.

"Hey, you don't know that. Wait, someone just picked up." He pointed to the phone he was holding.

"Hello, Doc? This is Vince Marotti, Jen's husband."

"Yeah, I'm fine. But my wife isn't. She's bleeding."

There was a pause while he received instructions. "OK," he said. "We'll meet you there."

He clicked off the phone and turned to his wife. "Come on, honey. He's going to meet us at the hospital."

The nurse had already taken her into a cubicle in the Emergency Room and helped her into one of those ridiculous hospital gowns by the time the doctor arrived. In spite of Vince's efforts, Jen couldn't stop crying.

"Jen. Lie down. Let's see what's going on here." Dr. Stefano's calm demeanor helped a little.

He pressed his hand on her abdomen. "The baby hasn't dropped," he said. "Some women do bleed during pregnancy, you know."

"I never heard of that," Jen said. "They do?"

The Secret Monster Within

"Yep," he said with a smile. "And it looks like you are one of them." He stripped the rubber gloves off and held her hand. "You're OK, Jen. The baby is fine."

"Are you sure?"

"I swear it," he said. "Just don't do anything too strenuous, or lift anything too heavy. Take it easy for the next two months, and you'll be fine."

"I'm not losing the baby?"

"No, honey. You're not. Just do as I said and make an appointment with my nurse for two weeks from now. We'll keep a close eye on you but I know you'll be fine."

Honest," he said when he saw the worry lines hadn't disappeared from her face. "I swear it," he averred with raised hand.

Jen managed a hint of a smile.

***

She almost lost the baby. Would that have made it easier for you? It doesn't matter anymore. You've waited too long, too long, too long. Get it done! The Monster was becoming very impatient.

Chapter 33

Vince was hired in the accounting department of a large manufacturing company located on Oak Street in downtown Buffalo, not too far from the waterfront. It was quite a distance from Amherst, but the thruway made the commute easy.

He had really liked his telephone-soliciting job, and found it difficult to give up, but the new one had a guaranteed salary and a chance for advancement. No more living just for today or just for himself. It was time to grow up and plan for the future. He had a wife and a soon-to-be-here baby to think about now.

And it couldn't have come at a more opportune time. Jen kept insisting she could manage at work, but Vince knew how often she was forced to pick up a fairly heavy child or bend over to help one. He had spent days begging her to quit work. "You heard what the doctor said," he reminded her. "Some women have to spend the whole nine months in bed. You really can't complain if you have to spend the little time you have left resting at home."

He thought of another bonus. "Donna will keep you company. And I'm sure Mrs. Longfellow...whoops, I mean Melanie...will understand. You don't want to take a chance on losing the baby. You know how you felt last week when you thought that you had."

Oh, yes. She would never forget it.

"I suppose you're right," she said. "I just hope I don't lose my job because of this. You have to admit that it's the perfect career for me after the baby is born. No baby sitter costs since the baby will be with me, and I'll be working at a place that I know and like. Not to mention, I just got a raise. I don't want to lose this job, Vin." She frowned at the thought of it.

"Talk to Melanie, hon. Maybe you can work something out with her."

Melanie Longfellow was most obliging. "Of course, Jen," she said. "I would never forgive myself if you lost the baby because of something you did here." Melanie Longfellow could easily be Jennifer's grandmother, both in looks and in actions. Her face crinkled into a sympathetic smile as she reached for Jen's hand.

"I promise you that your job will be here for you when you are able to return. The children love you. I'll simply hire a temporary till then." She continued smiling and encouraged Jen to take it easy. "I'll be looking forward to hearing about the birth of your baby. And don't forget, six months later, I'll be expecting you to show up for work." Melanie Longfellow tried to look gruff without much success.

"Thanks, Melanie. I'm looking forward to that day." Jen smiled.

Donna was happy to have Jen home during the day, and even offered to fit in more art classes during the week. But even with that, and a TV and a computer, life was boring. I miss being out with people and doing things, she thought. Just a couple more months now, she advised the baby hiding in her abdomen.

***

Now how are you going to do it, the Monster asked him?
I don't know, he screamed back.

Chapter 34

"It's been so quiet for so long. Do you suppose we're done with him?" Dan looked at Bernie with raised eyebrows.

"I'd sure like to think so, but you never know." The chief of police shook his head and rolled his eyes. He was as perplexed as any of them.

Bernie and Dan had become even closer since the holidays. They found it easy to talk to each other, and they shared bits and pieces about their jobs, their family members, and their lives.

Bernie raised his glass of Merlot in a form of a toast. "Here's to no more Monster."

"Hey, I'll drink to that!" Dan laughed as he raised his glass of wine also. They were eating at Pietros, one of their favorite Italian restaurants.

"Umm. This is good," Dan said as he put the forkful of twirled spaghetti in his mouth.

"You can say that again. I could eat Italian every night and not mind it one bit." Bernie filled his mouth with a large bite of his cheese lasagna. "I just hope I have enough room left when I finish this for that Napoleon I've been eyeing. My mouth is watering just thinking of it. I definitely should have been Italian!" He chuckled. "Here's to the Italians," he said, as he raised his glass once more, "and to their delicious food."

"I'll drink to that too." Dan laughed.

The spell was shattered by the sound of Bernie's ring tone.

And that was the end of dinner.

***

Catherine Stevens had sleek dark hair and green eyes, which explained her nickname of Cat, but because she was so tiny, some jokingly called her Kitty. She answered to both, as long as they were ordering food or drink. It didn't matter to her. She had been the sole proprietor of Kit-Cat's Restaurant for over a year now, and it was already doing a land-office business. Its location on the Buffalo waterfront didn't hurt either.

"Hey Cat. How about another round here?" Her good friend, Al Scully, stood and caught her attention.

Cat glanced at the clock before replying. "It's almost closing time, Al." The room was empty except for Al's table and one lone customer eating a hamburger.

"It won't take us long. Promise." Al laughed, as did the four fellows sitting at the table with him.

Cat smiled and nodded an OK.

The Secret Monster Within

Actually, she was grateful that Al and his friends were there. There was something just not right about the man sitting in the corner. His brown eyes bore holes into her as she went about her business. It gave her the creeps.

All five men blew her kisses when she delivered five foaming beers to Al's table. She was well liked by all her patrons, which helped explain the success of her fairly new business. It was such a pleasant change from her *last life* as Cat was prone to call it.

Cat had been married to a domineering control freak who seemed to enjoy sucking the life out of her. It was as far from a marriage made in heaven as you could get. Actually it was hell, but still it took her two years to work up the resolve to go it alone. She left him in Sacramento and flew back to her hometown of Buffalo, where her family welcomed her with open arms. One year later the divorce was final and she was giddy with feelings of liberation. She later heard via the grapevine that her ex had remarried, and all she could feel was sympathy for his new wife.

On the other hand, she had found a new love, one who was as different from her first as anyone could be. Sometimes she had to mentally pinch herself to see if she was dreaming, then she would smile and count her blessings: the perfect man who was soon to be her perfect husband, and she was back home in Buffalo, where she had been born and raised. Life just couldn't get any better.

Plus, she loved the business she was in. She had come to know the families who felt comfortable in bringing their children to the restaurant area of her business, and the working men who frequented her restaurant and bar as well. They had all become good friends, and she treasured each and every one of them.

All, that is, except this one hamburger-eating man. He left the money on the table and walked out without saying a word. Cat breathed a sigh of relief. She was more than grateful that he had left before Al and his friends. Now she felt safe.

She busied herself cleaning up and getting ready to close.

"Hey, Cat. Thanks a million, hon." Al was his loud and jovial self. The five men brought their dirty glasses to the counter and threw her another kiss.

"You're welcome, guys. See you tomorrow?" Cat beamed at them.

"You betcha. So long." They all answered at once.

"Bye. See you then." Cat locked the door after them and resumed her cleaning chores. They were almost done so it wouldn't take long now.

The usual lunch crowd was waiting for the door to be opened. It was a good hour past Cat's usual opening time. "What gives?" Everyone was perplexed. Some leaned on their car's horn, while others knocked on the glass doors of the still-dark restaurant. It was plain that no one was in there. "Where could she be?" Obviously there was not to be any lunch at Kit-Cats today, and her steady customers left shaking their heads and shrugging their shoulders.

Now it was nearing dinnertime, and the dark restaurant said it all. No longer satisfied with questioning themselves, one of her steady customers took it upon himself to call the police.

"What do you mean we have to wait forty-eight hours?" he asked. "Cat's always here. Something has happened." Bob Hutton wouldn't take no for an answer.

"Oh, what the hell." Capt. Shepherd figured it wouldn't hurt to send the squad car that usually patrolled the waterfront area to check it out.

The Secret Monster Within

They found her body in the trash bin behind her restaurant, and it bore the secret signature of The Monster.

"I should have known it was too good to be true," Bernie said as he stared into the unseeing green eyes of the dead girl.

"Damn." Dan backed away to let forensics get closer to her.

Their friend, Capt. Barry Shepherd, had called them the minute he saw the body and the identifying mark of The Monster. It was his precinct, but he knew this was their case as well.

It was as they knew it would be—there were no clues, no DNA, no anything. How could this monster do these despicable acts of violence and never leave a clue? Was he some kind of a magician? Bernie was beginning to wonder.

***

Sharon was getting tired of the police protection, but was afraid of losing it. She knew they wouldn't, they couldn't, spend a lifetime providing it. Bernie Roper had told her there was only so much money in the budget and it was being stretched to the limit as it was. How much longer could they do it? And what would she do when it was no longer available? She didn't want to think about it.

As she read the newspaper, she took a deep breath of relief. She felt sorry for the dead girl, but it hadn't been her. Her hands shook as she folded the paper.

***

That was good, the monster said. But it wasn't Jen

Chapter 35

Jen backed up so she might see it better. "Wow. Did I do that?"

"You sure did, Jennifer Marotti. I'm saying your name because some day it might become famous." Donna laughed.

"Yeah, sure." Jen laughed with her. "But it sure looks good to me."

"Well, you know what? It looks good to me, too." Donna nodded her head. "And I don't give out accolades very easily." She raised her eyebrows and smiled. "You've come a long way, baby."

The painting was a still life of a bowl of fruit and some flowers.

"The colors are vibrant. No muddy fruit in there,"

The Secret Monster Within

Donna said. "You've done a beautiful job for your first one, Jen. I'm proud of you."

"Well, thanks, but the credit all goes to you. You are a wonderful teacher. Believe me when I say that."

"Teaching would be easy if all students were like you."

"Hey, what is this? A mutual admiration society?" Vince had entered Donna's art studio without a sound.

"Oh, Vin, you're here." Jennifer was pleased at the surprise visit and couldn't hide the pride she was feeling. "Look what I've done," she said as she backed away so Vince could better see her painting.

"Wow," he said. "You've really got talent, honey. That looks great."

"Think so? I love doing it." Jen beamed and then turned to Donna once more. "Donna, I can't thank you enough for giving me this golden opportunity. I never would have known I had it in me if you hadn't taken me on. Gratis, I might add."

"And speaking of that," Jen continued, "I'm hoping that when I return to work, we'll be able to pay you."

"Don't worry about it, Jen. We'll see when the time comes. Right now, you've given me all I could ask for." Donna pointed at the finished piece of art. "You might even have encouraged me to take up teaching art."

"Oh, I wish you would. You are a wonderful teacher and whoever gets you will be so lucky. I know I am." Jen clasped her hands to her heart.

"Well, you'll always be my number one student." Donna smiled.

***

"What's for dinner?" Vince laughed.

Jen joined in the merriment. "Well, you have your

choice. Would you like Southwestern Chicken, or Meatloaf, or Pot Roast, or...." Jen lifted the boxes of frozen food in the small freezer that rested in a corner of her bedroom and joined in the laughter.

"Pot roast," Vin said as quickly as that. "Haven't had that for at least five days now."

"I feel so guilty," Jen said. "But with only a microwave, what can I do? I promise I'll learn to cook as soon as we get a place and I get a stove. Honest."

"Hey. We get one good meal at your folks' house every Sunday, and I honest-to-God do like these TV dinners. And I'm not kidding," he said as he pursed his lips for a kiss.

"Oh, Vin. You're such a good guy," she said as she kissed him. "Better days are coming."

Chapter 36

"What?" Bernie sat up straight in his office chair. "You're kidding." He looked across his desk at Dan with wide eyes, and then laid the phone in its cradle. His mouth was still agape.

"What is it?" Dan asked. He could see it was something big.

"Shep's been questioning everyone that hangs around the waterfront and, voila." Bernie's eyes opened wide and a grin went from ear to ear.

"Voila? Bernie, what is it?

"They've found a homeless man who saw an unidentified car parked near the restaurant the same night that Catherine Stevens was murdered. Not far from the area where the body was found."

Dan's shoulders sagged in disappointment. "What's news about that?" Dan shook his head. "Wouldn't there be lots of cars parked there? I mean it's a popular restaurant, Bernie." He hated to crush his friend's newfound enthusiasm, but this was crazy.

"No, no. I mean after-hours. After the restaurant was closed for the night. There's no other business near there." Bernie's mouth formed a straight line of determination, and he balled his hands into two fists and shook them. "There's no reason for any car other than Catherine Stevens' to be there after the restaurant has closed."

His smile said it all.

Dan stared at him with open mouth. "Oh, my God, Bernie, that is good news. He didn't get the license plate number, did he? Nah," he flicked his hand in a dismissive way. "He wouldn't have. Would he?" His brow crinkled with hope.

"Dan, he did. I couldn't believe it either, but it seems this fellow likes to make up words from the first three letters of the licenses he sees. This one was BDD, and he found it easy to remember because he made up the phrase Big Drug Dealer."

"Wonder where he came up with that one," Dan said with a sneer.

"Well, who the hell cares," Bernie said with a laugh. "Just thank God he did. He got the three letters *and* the full three numbers that followed because they were in sequence. I mean, Dan, we got the whole damn license plate number! Can you believe it?"

Bernie was so excited, he couldn't sit still. He made a fist of victory and rose from his chair. "Yes, we've got him!" He spit it out with a vengeance and started pacing the floor.

"Dan, the car is registered to a Carlos Rodriguez."

The Secret Monster Within

Bernie took a deep breath and came back to his desk, but couldn't sit down. "The police are bringing him in as we speak, and Shep's coming too." Bernie could barely contain himself.

"Carlos Rodriguez?" It was obvious Dan was trying to remember where he had heard that name before. "I know that name, but I can't place it."

"We'll find out soon enough, Dan." Ben shook his head as if awakening from a bad dream. "Can you believe it? We're finally going to meet The Monster. What a red letter day this is." They shook hands and then clapped each other on the back.

***

The two-way mirror revealed the man who they now knew was The Monster, although he certainly didn't look like one. They each reluctantly agreed that the clothes he wore were obviously more expensive than any of them could afford and his hair was nicely trimmed. One of the police officers even made note of the fact that his nails were neatly manicured and polished. His large puppy dog eyes could have fooled almost anyone, but through the years, both Dan and Bernie had seen enough murderers who didn't look the part, so appearances meant nothing to them.

"He looks bewildered, but not nervous. I wonder why?" There were worry lines between Dan's eyes.

"I don't know," Bernie said, "but let's see what we can do about that."

Capt. Shepherd stayed behind to watch through the mirror while Dan and Bernie entered the interrogation room together.

"Hello, Mr. Rodriguez," Bernie said with the hint of a smile. Dan scowled at him. Good cop, bad cop?

"What the hell am I doing here?" Carlos Rodriguez was full of indignant wrath.

"Well, that's what we aim to find out," Bernie replied. "You look like an educated, up-to-date sort of a man. I don't have to tell you about the girl who was found murdered on the waterfront a few days ago, do I? Catherine Stevens?"

"What? Well, of course not. It's all over the news. But what has that got to do with me?" Carlos Rodriguez was becoming very agitated.

"That's what we aim to find out." Bernie glared into Carlos's eyes.

"What's this all about?" Carlos looked genuinely confused. "I demand to know. Do I need a lawyer?"

"You certainly are entitled to one, and you're allowed one phone call. I suggest you use it wisely. Here's a phone. We'll be waiting outside." Bernie rose and Dan followed.

They shut the door and peered through the two-way mirror. "Damn. I was hoping he'd let something slip." Dan used his fist to punch his other hand in a show of irritation.

"Well, we have to go by the book, Dan. We don't want to lose our prime suspect on a technicality."

"That's for sure." Dan was quick to agree.

They listened while Carlos called his lawyer and watched him lose his patience when he was told the lawyer wasn't in just then.

"He's got a cell phone but I don't have that number with me," he informed the answering service. "Call him right now and tell him that Dr. Carlos Rodriguez is at the Amherst Police Station. I'm being held on suspicion of murder. Did you get that?" he screamed at the top of his lungs. "Murder!" He shook his head as if trying to wake up

The Secret Monster Within

from a bad dream.

Dan and Bernie both heard him mutter, "This can't be happening" as he hung up the phone. Then they entered the interrogation room once more.

"I'm not saying anything till my lawyer comes." Carlos set his mouth in a thin line, and Dan knew he meant it.

***

"What was your car doing at the waterfront last Monday?" No sense beating around the bush. Bernie hoped that Carlos Rodriguez would be so shocked to learn that the police knew where he had been on the night of the murder that he might own up to it, lawyer or not.

Fred Flynn, his attorney, held up his hand in an effort to stop him from replying.

"What?" Carlos looked relieved. "Monday night?" he asked.

"Yeah. Monday night. The night that Catherine Stevens was murdered." Bernie's eyes were intense. We've got him, he thought.

"Oh, for crying out loud. I'd forgotten what day it happened on. I could have saved you and my lawyer a lot of time. I was responding to an emergency call at Gates Millard Fillmore Hospital Monday night. I'm a doctor. You can check with anyone who was at the hospital that evening."

"What?" Bernie looked at him with disbelieving eyes. "Your car was at the waterfront. We have an eyewitness who saw it there. He memorized the license plate number. You can't get out of this, Rodriguez."

"Well, looks like your eyewitness didn't have very good eyesight," Fred Flynn said. "It shouldn't be too hard to check on my client's alibi, should it?"

"No, it shouldn't," Bernie said, almost in a daze. How could this be happening?

It took but one quick call to Millard Fillmore Gates Circle Hospital to verify Carlos Rodriguez's alibi, and now they were back to square one.

"You know," Dan said, "the person who reported the car to us described the car as a deep blue Lexus. Your car is a deep blue Lexus. The license plate matches. There's something very fishy here, Carlos."

"Don't ask me about coincidences. All I know is I was at the hospital at the time in question. I can assure you, I am not a murderer. My vocation is saving lives, not taking them." His nose-in-the-air attitude was beginning to get on Dan's nerves.

"Well, maybe you weren't there, but your car sure as hell was."

"Sorry. My car hasn't learned to drive itself!" He turned to his lawyer and suggested they leave.

"Wait a minute," Bernie said. "Did you loan your car to anyone that night?"

Both he and Dan noted the brief hesitation.

"N..no." Rodriguez's bushy black eyebrows almost met in the middle of his forehead as he gathered his face into a worried frown. "No, I didn't."

"You don't seem too sure about that, Carlos." Dan glared at him.

"Well, I am. I wasn't there. My car wasn't there. And at this point, I'm sick of being here. Ready, Fred?" Carlos stood and was ready to leave.

"Hey! Who said we're done with you? Sit down." Dan stood so his entire six foot three inch height was in full view.

A much shorter Carlos obediently sat without a word of protest.

The Secret Monster Within

"You said you were at the hospital from nine till approximately one AM. Right?" Bernie leaned forward, waiting for the answer, even though he knew what it was going to be.

"Yes. That's right."

"Where do you park your car while on duty at the hospital?"

"In the doctors' parking lot, right behind to the hospital."

"And that's where you parked it Monday night?"

"Of course."

"All right," Bernie continued. "Can you deny that there is a chance that someone got your car started, with a key or without, and 'borrowed' it for the evening?" He used his two index fingers to denote the quote.

"What?" Carlos looked incredulous. "Stole my car? I can't imagine such a thing."

"You can't?" Dan scoffed.

"Well, I suppose...." Carlos looked at his lawyer.

"Of course that could happen." Fred Flynn was only too happy to give birth to this notion. "In fact, I'm sure that must be what did happen. Your car with your license plate was found at the waterfront while you were on hospital duty. How else can we explain it?"

"Tell me, Carlos. Was your car in the same space when you came out of work as when you went in?" Dan was working him too.

"I'm almost sure it was," he answered hesitantly. "Of course, it could have been one space this way or that. I didn't pay that much attention when I parked it. Late afternoons and evenings are not as crowded so there are plenty of parking spaces available, unlike earlier in the day or just after dinner."

"OK, Dr. Rodriquez, we know you weren't at the waterfront last Monday, but I'd almost stake my life on the fact that your car was. We'll have to confiscate it to look for clues. I'm sure you understand." Bernie rose to signify the questioning period was over.

"How am I supposed to get to work?"

"Have you ever heard of Enterprise or Hertz?"

"Rent a car?" Carlos looked at him in disbelief.

"You'd be surprised how many people do that, Dr. Rodriguez. We aren't keeping your car forever. We'll take good care of it, promise. Mr. Flynn can drive you home now. Right?" Bernie looked at the lawyer.

"Of course. Come on, Carlos. We'll get the paper work for your car and be on our way."

"That car is my pride and joy. It had been come back to me in the same condition it's in now. Or else!" Carlos turned in disgust.

Dan and Bernie exchanged glances and shrugged their shoulders.

***

Nina Rodriguez's coal black eyes spit fire. "Where have you been?" she demanded.

"I left you a note. Didn't you see it?" Carlos fought to keep his voice calm

"Yes. I saw it. What the heck does *Gone on an errand* mean? You've been gone for hours. A phone call wouldn't hurt, you know." Nina Rodriguez was full of rage and indignation.

"I didn't want to spell it out. I was afraid Karen would see it. We don't need employees spreading rumors before they know all the facts."

"Karen? Since when did you consider Karen an employee? She's been our housekeeper for over twenty years

The Secret Monster Within

now. You know she's family. What are you talking about?"

"Nina. Sit down. You're not going to believe what I have to tell you."

Nina took a deep breath and fought for control. She sat on a kitchen chair. "This had better be good," she said with a look that pretty much indicated she was sure it wouldn't be.

"The police were here today. I had to go down to the station with them."

"What?" She was incredulous. "What for?"

"Here's the real kicker." Carlos reached across the table to hold her hand. "My car was seen at the waterfront the same day they discovered that dead girl's body there."

"Oh, for crying out loud. What kind of story are you handing me?" Nina shook her head in disbelief.

"I'm not kidding. A hobo saw my car and memorized the license plate number. My car was there the night that girl was murdered."

"Carlos. What are you saying? How could your car have been there?"

"Well, they now know that I was working at the hospital that night. They know I wasn't there. But they also know my car was." Carlos read the question in his wife's eyes.

"They think someone might have stolen it from the parking ramp and brought it back before I knew it was missing."

"When was all this supposed to have happened?" Nina's pretty face was fraught with fear.

"Monday night. The night Catherine Stevens was murdered."

"Monday night?" A deep line creased her forehead as she thought back.

"Wait! Carlos. Wasn't that the night..." Carlos put his

finger on her lips to silence her.
"Carlos. That was the night...."
"Shhh. Let them think what they want to think."
"But you can't..."
"Yes, I can. Enough! I'm off the hook. Leave well enough alone."

Chapter 37

Before Jen and Vince were married, the miniscule combination of their individual income, plus no savings account, had netted each an unsatisfactory credit rating. But now, in spite of Jen's maternity leave, they were both on the books as having full-time jobs, and they were a married couple. This, plus a savings account they had started with their wedding money, upped their credit rating to that of *Satisfactory*.

"I think it's time we started looking for a house." Vince had just checked all the figures.

"What?" Jen stared at him wide-eyed. "Do you think we have enough money to buy a house?"

Vince could sense Jen's eagerness.

"Hey, we've got a good solid base now." Vince pressed

his hands in the sign of prayer. "Just thank God we both agreed to put the rest of our wedding money into a bank account for a down payment on a house." He crinkled his nose at her. "You were even willing to give up getting a car right away for this very reason. Kudos to you, Jen."

"Oh, Vinnie. Wouldn't that be wonderful?" Jen's eyes gleamed with happiness.

Vince smiled as he squeezed her hand. "It sure would be, honey. Let's go to the bank and find out."

The news was good, and Jen could barely wait to get back to their apartment and start looking for their first house. Buffalo's property values had never gone through the wild up and down cycles that other US cities had gone through, but it had slowly inched up enough that Vince and Jen knew they had to shop very carefully.

"We can't start at the top. We'll have plenty of time for that," they assured each other. So it would have to be a smaller and older home, but it would be new to them.

On the downside, they would hate leaving Donna and Rob. They had both grown so close to their landlords that they now considered them good friends, and they knew how much they would miss them. But it didn't take a mental giant to realize there would be no room for a married couple and their new baby in their current one-bedroom apartment. Even Donna and Rob had reluctantly conceded as much.

At the beginning, looking for a house was fun. Their very own house! Jen was elated, and though Vince tried to look cool, he couldn't hide the excitement he felt about this new venture.

It went without saying that they would live in Amherst, but it took only days for them to realize there were no givens in life. "There isn't anything on the Amherst market right now that is in our price range." Jen was forced to concede defeat.

"So what?" Vince reassured her with a smile and a shrug. "What's wrong with Cheektowaga or Tonawanda. There are some really nice homes in our price range in both those suburbs. We don't have to live in Amherst, you know."

"Oh, we don't have to? How do I get to work?" Had he forgotten already?

"I've been thinking about that. If we move to either one of these nearby affordable towns, we could lease a small car for you. With both of us working, we can afford that till we save up enough to buy a used one later on. What do you think?"

Jen nodded her head. "Sounds good to me, and I'd love to have a car again!" She laughed with joyous excitement. "I can't wait to call Dorothy and tell her she can start looking in those other areas. I think she'll be happy too."

Dorothy Wallace was their realtor and she had hinted more than once that Amherst was not the place for newlyweds that were in Vince and Jen's income bracket to be looking. She allowed that there were smaller and older homes that came on the Amherst market, but they were rare.

"I'm almost certain she'll find us something we can afford in these other towns a whole lot quicker." Jen was almost giddy with delight.

"Most definitely," Vince assured her.

"And she'd better. Maybe you haven't noticed," she rubbed her nose against Vince's, "but we don't have a whole lot of time left." Jen stepped back and pointed at her nearly full term belly.

"Oh, I've noticed," Vince said with a laugh, as he hugged her the best he could.

Margaret McMillen

***

Jen's face glowed with happiness. She had always enjoyed baby showers because they were for such a happy occasion, but this one was even more special. Melanie had insisted on giving this one for her and Vince's baby, and Jen was on cloud nine.

"I just love this!" she exclaimed over every gift she opened. And the truth was, she did. The sweet little garments, the practical gifts, all of them. Of course, since the baby's gender was still unknown, everything was in white or green or yellow, three of Jen's favorite colors. All would match the colors she had used for the nursery in the new house they had just bought.

"I am just so full of happiness, it should be illegal," she told the guests. "As you know, Vince and I just bought a new house, and we'll soon have a new baby. What more could anyone ask for?" She held her hands in prayer form and raised her eyes to give thanks. "I'm truly blessed."

"And in addition, I have all of you," she said as a sweep of her hands included all her dear friends and loved ones. "I know it's not fair, but I think I just might be the happiest woman alive."

Although Jen had already leased a car, Vince suggested that it might be a good idea to have him drive her both to and from the restaurant where the shower was being held. "You'll need help loading the car with all the gifts you'll be getting," he suggested with a smile. She readily agreed, and as it turned out, was happy he had thought of it.

"Wow. Looks like we hit the jackpot," he exclaimed, as he carried armfuls of gifts out to the car.

"Oh, Vin. Everyone was so generous. Our little one's not going to want for anything. I can't wait to put some of

The Secret Monster Within

these things in the nursery," she said as she used the seat belt extender to cover both her and her baby.

Their feelings of elation evaporated in a split second as they pulled into their driveway. Something or someone ran from the cover of bushes located next to their house.

"What was that?" Vince asked.

Jen put her hand over her heart and admitted she had no idea. "It scared me though."

"Yeah, me too." Vince got out of the car and opened the door for Jen while surveying the area. "You go in the house," he said. "I'll bring the gifts in."

"Oh, Vin. I can help."

"No! Into the house," he demanded. "Now!" Vince continued scanning the area, but it was dark and there was nothing to be seen.

"You come in too, Vin. We'll unload the presents tomorrow." The joy was gone and had been replaced with fear.

"If there's someone out here, do you want them to steal all your presents?" Vince tried to make light of it.

"Well, it would have to be someone who's going to have a baby." Jen's laugh broke the spell.

"You're right." Vince smiled back in an attempt to reduce Jen's fear. "Nevertheless, take this bag. I'll bring the rest in."

"OK," Jen conceded. "I can't wait to start putting these in the nursery."

"Then get to it, girl. I'll be right in." Vince waved her on.

The weather was warming up. In fact, it was almost stifling, but they both agreed not to open any windows. "Glad we got these room air conditioners," he said.

"Me, too."

"Oh, Vin. I love our house, don't you?"

"It's a good starter home. Yes, I like it." Vince looked around as if seeing it for the first time. It was only four rooms plus a bath, but it was all they needed. Both of them had fallen in love with the huge eat-in kitchen that came with all appliances furnished, the nice-sized living room, and the two large bedrooms. It had a full basement, with one half of it devoted to laundry facilities, furnace and storage, and the other half, sporting a finished rec room.

And best yet, it didn't show it's age even though it was almost sixty years old. The last owners had replaced the old worn shingles with white vinyl siding and light blue trim so its up-to-date exterior was maintenance free, and it had a matching two-car garage that was just a few feet from the back door. Jen liked the colors, and was especially fond of the large front porch.

"They don't make 'em like that anymore," their agent had reminded them. "And it's a shame they don't. You'll love sitting out here on a warm summer's eve, sipping a couple of lemonades and talking with your neighbors. And you do have that small deck on the back too."

Both Jen and Vince had rejoiced in the fact that they had found their new home in a heavily treed neighborhood in Tonawanda, a suburb adjacent to Amherst, and not that far from Playground for Kids. In fact, everything had been perfect.

But now, what creature was lurking outside, snatching that happiness away from them? Vince positioned the phone on the nightstand next to him, within easy reach.

Chapter 38

Sharon had to admit her nerves were getting the better of her. She found sleeping was a luxury that was almost impossible to obtain without the use of a sleeping pill, and her nerves caused her stomach to roil every time she ate. She was losing weight, and the dark circles under her eyes were aging her by the minute. This maniac is killing me inch by inch, she admitted to herself. Something's got to be done, but what?

Every day, if she was lucky enough to finally fall asleep, she awoke with a knot her stomach. Every day she lived in fear. No human could take this for long, and it had already been much too long, with months and months of worry. Sometimes she found herself almost wishing that the Monster had finished her off in the parking lot. At least it would have been quick and over and done with. This was a tortuously slow death.

And the trips out of town were no relief either. He could follow her, wherever she went. She knew that. He knew who she was, he knew where she worked, and he knew where she lived. The constancy of always being on the alert was slowly eating the life out of her, not to mention the promise of a successful career at Acme. Even that was suffering, and she knew it. But what could she do?

***

Richard had been most considerate after she returned from Florida. He knew what she was going through and he did all he could to make it easier for her. But there's only so much an employer can do, and business is business.

"We may have to let Sharon go," Richard told his boss.

Alan Casey shook his head in disbelief. "She's one of our best," he was quick to point out.

"Humph. Don't I know it." Richard closed his eyes and clenched his jaw. "But look at her record since The Monster attacked her." Richard pointed to the papers in front of them.

"I know. I've seen them. But this is one very unusual circumstance." Alan slapped the report with his open palm. "We've got to give her more time."

"Hey, you're the boss. If you want to, that's fine with me. My heart goes out to her too, but you've got to realize how this reflects on my record. The higher-ups don't know Sharon or what she's going through. All they know is one of my employees isn't doing her job, and that makes me look bad. You've got to see my point, Alan."

"I do. But believe me, the higher-ups have been informed as to her unique circumstances and have given me

The Secret Monster Within

the green light to give her a little more time. This can't last forever."

"Can't it?" Richard made a wry face. "This guy's been getting away with murder for years now," Richard reminded him. "How many years are Frank and Eric going to be so generous?" Frank Waterman and Eric Nieswander had started this business not that many years ago, and they had been the team that got it off the ground. Richard had risen to where he was by hanging on to their coattails and wasn't about to throw his career opportunities away because of one girl.

"How about some psychological help for Sharon?" Alan looked at Richard with a gleam of hope in his eyes.

"She's already going to one. Hasn't done any good yet, as you can see." Richard shook his head as he pointed at the reports again.

"Well, we'll give her a little more time. Keep me informed." Alan's nod indicated the meeting was over.

"You've got it. Sharon's lucky to have a guy like you in charge."

"Well, I don't know if it's luck or not, but I've got a daughter just about Sharon's age, and I know how I'd feel if The Monster was after her." Alan shuddered at the thought. "Oh, God. What a cruel fate."

"You can say that again." Richard picked up the report and turned to leave.

***

He knew she wasn't eating and he watched her growing thinner. He saw the darkening circles and knew she wasn't sleeping. This form of torture was new to him, and it was fun. Sure, he could end it anytime he wanted to, but this was a slow death, a whole new experience. Why rush it?

Chapter 39

Renee Shuster loved to dance. The only fault she could find with her lessons was they were over too soon. An hour and a half, twice a week, just weren't enough, at least not for her. She closed her eyes and dreamt of what it would be like to have a career as a dancer. Imagine doing something one loved so much and receiving payment for it as well. Oh, what a life that would be.

"Got that Viola account finished yet?"

"Huh? Oh, yes, Rex. I'm sorry. Daydreaming." She grimaced. "Here it is." She smiled at Rex Weber as she handed the report to him. He was such a nice guy, and she was so lucky to have found this job right after high school graduation. The pay was good, and most of her friends envied her.

The Secret Monster Within

"What's it like to work for a guy as handsome as Rex Weber?" "What's he like?" "Is he married?" "Any chance he may be interested in you?" Everyone had a million questions.

"Yes," she would patiently answer, "he is married, and it's fun to work for him. He's one of the nicest men I've ever met. And no, he's not interested in me. Not at all." Why in the world would anyone think that this tall, handsome Adonis would be interested in her? "I'm too short, I'm too dark, and I'm too French," she would tell them. "Well, at least the Renee part of me is." And then she would laugh.

She had been working at Johnson and Johnson for almost ten years now, and had worked her way up from the typing pool to the esteemed position of Secretary to the Vice-President. Johnson and Johnson were father and son, lawyers to the core. The two-man business has grown and blossomed to the large conglomerate it was today, and her title and position were nothing to sneeze at. But she'd give it all up in a minute if she could be a professional dancer, in a minute.

"Thanks, Renee. You did a great job," he said as he leafed through the papers. "But it's getting late now." Rex glanced at the clock. "Time for you to be heading home. See you Monday."

"OK, Rex. Have a nice weekend."

Rex Weber's smile should be outlawed. "Thanks. You too," he said. He returned her wave as she left.

She hadn't realized just how late it was until she stepped outside and saw the summer light was already fading. The faint orange hue of the western sky told her she had missed another beautiful sunset. Oh well, what else have I got to do? Summer TV stinks, and there was no one waiting for her at her apartment, not even a pet since they weren't allowed in her complex. Someday, she thought once again. Someday I'll have a home and kids and lots of cats and dogs to make up for these lonely days.

But I'm almost thirty, she reminded herself. Better get a-moving. That was her mother's favorite advice, and it was beginning to make sense.

It was a long drive from downtown Buffalo to her apartment in Amherst, but she always enjoyed the view from the northbound Thruway. The Niagara River that ran alongside it was dotted with small watercraft, sailboats, and yachts, and it was a narrow river so you could see the lighted homes of the Canadian residents.

It was Friday and so it was eat-out night in Buffalo and its surrounding suburbs. It was difficult to find a spot at any restaurant on Fridays, but especially those that served Buffalo's famous fish fries. Renee had traveled extensively and knew there was no other place on earth where they served such good fish dinners for such a reasonable price as that of her hometown.

And who wanted to cook fish in their own home? Certainly not Renee. The fish smell and the grease mess made it a most disagreeable chore.

But, it was late. Most of the restaurants would be through serving their notable dinner, and what was left, may not be worth the stop. Eat out, eat at home, she wavered back and forth, knowing full well she didn't have much time to think about it if she wanted to exit at the Colvin ramp that would take her to her favorite fish place.

What have I got to cook at home at this ungodly hour? Yes, fish fry, it is. She got in the right lane and made the proper off ramp just in time.

"Hey, look at the time." Johnny Fieldstone pointed at his watch. "Almost ready to close up the kitchen, you know."

The Secret Monster Within

"I realize that, Johnny. If you can't make a fish fry, I certainly understand. Got held up at the office." She smiled at the owner of her favorite restaurant. "I'll find something to make at home. There's always peanut butter and jelly." Now she laughed out loud.

"You want me to live with the guilt? No way, Jose. We'll get you a fish fry, hon. I wouldn't be able to sleep tonight knowing I had sent you home to p and j." Johnny joined in the laughter.

"I'll remember this. Thanks, Johnny."

It didn't take long, but then, deep-fried fish usually doesn't. And it was hot and crisp and delicious as always.

"How is it?" Johnny asked.

"Umm." That's all she needed to say.

It was completely dark now, and the summer sky sparkled with twinkling stars that outshone the sliver of moon that appeared overhead.

Renee pulled her car into the reserved spot she had requested just this year. She liked this back row parking as a wooded area edged it, thereby cutting down on the chance of scratches and dents from other cars and pedestrians. In spite of the fact that everyone thought she was crazy to have given up the preferred front row spot she previously owned, she was sure she had done the right thing. "I don't mind those few extra steps if it means a few less dents," she had laughingly told all those who questioned her choice.

She exited her car and had just turned to go into her apartment when she heard a voice calling out to her.

"Excuse me."

There was a distinguished looking gentleman sitting in the passenger side of the car parked next to her.

"Yes?" she replied.

"My wife and I are new here, and we're looking to find

a place to live. She's just gone in to the office. Do you live here?" he asked.

"Why, yes, I do."

"How do you like it here? In these apartments, I mean."

"I like it just fine. We have really nice neighbors, and the apartments have everything you could ask for."

"Washers and dryers?"

"Oh, yes," she said.

The well-dressed gentleman opened his car door and started to get out. "Maybe I should go in with my wife and see what they have to offer."

"Oh, I would if I were you," Renee assured him.

"You've been most kind and helpful," he told her.

"No problem," she said as she turned to walk to the entrance of her complex.

***

The found her body in the woods two days later.

Chapter 40

"You know, I really like this house." Jen spread her arms and turned to include all four rooms in her assessment of their tiny new home.

"I'm glad you're so easy to please." Vince laughed at her.

"It's enough for us. Even for this little one," Jen said as she pointed to her very pregnant tummy. "Don't you just love the way the nursery looks?"

"Yes I do, honey. You did a great job on it."

"Well, you helped. You did all the painting. And a beautiful job it was, too."

"Well, thank you, Mam. My motto is I aim to please."

Jen rose on here tiptoes and kissed her husband. "You certainly do please me."

"Really?" Vince said with a leer.

"Yes. Although it's just a vague memory now." Jen rolled her eyes as they both counted the days they had been told to refrain from sex. "Hope I remember how to do it when we get the OK."

"Hey, it's just like riding a bicycle. Well, you know what I mean." They were getting silly.

"Yeah, I know what you mean. Come here you yum yum." As Jen reached up to hug him, she suddenly recoiled as if someone had hit her in the belly.

"Jen! What's the matter?" Vince's face creased with concern.

"Oh, nothing. It was just a quick pain. It's gone now. Must have been all those French fries I ate."

Vince chuckled and waved a naughty finger at her.

"Anything on TV tonight?" Vince picked up the paper to look at the TV news.

"I'm not crazy about Friday nights. Maybe we should have looked into going to a movie. Or getting one."

Vince shrugged. "If you want, we can run down and rent one now."

"Yeah. Let's do that. Let me get a drink of water first though. I'm so thirsty from all that salt and fat. But that fish fry sure was good." Jen turned to go to the kitchen, and suddenly doubled over. "Ooof."

"Jen! What's the matter?" Vince rushed to her side.

"Oh, Vince. Another terrible pain."

"Honey. Come sit down. I think you've started labor." Vince put his arm around her and led her to the sofa.

"Labor? Oh, no." He could see the fear in her eyes. "I'm scared," she admitted.

"Hey, we aren't sure what it is yet, but if it turns out to be labor, I'll be with you all the way. Just relax while I call the doctor." Vince gave her a quick kiss and picked up the phone.

The Secret Monster Within

The phone seemed to ring forever. It was finally picked up by an answering service.

Vince wrote something on a piece of paper and hung the phone back in its cradle. "The answering service says if it's an emergency I should call this number." He pointed to the paper he was holding.

"Wait, Vince. I've only had two pains so far. I think I'd better give it a little more time. But save that number just in case Dr. Stefano isn't back when we need him." Jen sat on the couch and patted the cushion next to her, inviting Vince to join her.

When he did, he put his arm around her shoulders and pressed her to him. "Hey, Mommy," he whispered.

"Hi, Daddy." Jen's eyes showed signs of brimming.

"You'll be fine. By this time tomorrow night, we'll have It to take care of." Vince knew this would bring a smile.

And Jen didn't disappoint him. "I can't wait to meet It."

"Neither can I." Vince hugged her once more.

It took most of the night before Vince and Jen and their doctor agreed it was time to meet at the hospital, and it had been a long night with no sleep. Jen was exhausted but the pains were close now, and it wouldn't be long.

Suddenly she found herself grunting and bearing down. It seemed she had no say in it whatsoever. It just happened.

"Time for the delivery room." The doctor nodded his head at the nurses and attendants.

Jen was lost in a world of pain. There was no beginning and no end. She had never suffered so in her life. She strained and grunted and screamed for relief. "My God. My God," she cried.

"Breathe, honey." Vince held her hand and kissed her brow. "Remember how we practiced?"

Jen's panting ended in a huge bearing-down grunt. "Here comes the baby," the doctor informed them.

Jen felt a warm sense of relief, and heard her baby cry for the first time.

"You have a beautiful baby girl," the doctor informed them. "She's perfect." He was all smiles as he held up their new daughter.

Vince wiped the sweat from Jen's brow and kissed her once more. "Oh, honey, she's beautiful."

"Let me see her." Jen reached for the crying baby that was still wet from birth.

"Here," the nurse said as she took the newborn from the doctor's hands. "Let me clean her up a bit. Be right back." She took the baby while the doctor waited for the placenta. One more bearing-down pain, and it was over.

"Here she is, your lovely little girl." The nurse laid their baby in Jen's crooked arm.

"Oh, my gosh. She is beautiful, isn't she?" Jen stared at the profile of her newborn. "And look at all that black curly hair! Sorry, hon, but I think you got Nana's and my hair gene." She laughed and then kissed her baby.

"She's almost a pretty as you are." Vince smiled and bent to kiss them both.

***

You messed up. She's had her baby. What are you going to do now?

Nothing, Monster. I've done enough. Jen and her baby will live. Got it?

Nothing? That's what you think!

Chapter 41

"Carlos!" Nina stared at the TV, then turned to her husband. "You've got to tell them, Carlos. You've just got to."

The news of the latest victim was on all three local newscasts.

"But Nina. It couldn't be him."

Nina Rodriguez rolled her eyes. "That's up to them to find out, not us. You've got to tell them the truth. How many more young girls do you want to have murdered before you do the right thing?"

Carlos shook his head and closed his eyes. "But Nina, it couldn't be him. I just know it. And what kind of trouble would I be getting him into, and for nothing? It could ruin his whole life. Do you realize that?"

"Oh, my God, Carlos, I know how you feel. I find myself feeling the same way. I just know it couldn't be him, and yet," her voice faded, "how else do you explain it?"

"I don't know. I just don't know what to do." He bent his head in defeat.

Nina walked over to her husband and put her hand on his shoulder. Then she quietly said, "Pick up the phone, Carlos, and make that call."

***

Bernie sat as though in a trance, in fact, he felt as though he was. He still held the phone in his hand even though the caller had already hung up.

"Hello. Anybody home?" Dan laughed.

Bernie shook his head and stared at Dan with his mouth opened in astonishment.

"You're not going to believe it." Bernie finally hung the phone on the cradle, and shook his head once more. "You're not going to believe it!" Bernie's brow creased and his eyes spit fire.

Dan realized this was no joke.

"What is it, Bernie?" Dan had discarded the smiley face and turned to his friend, full of concern.

"Dan. That was Dr. Carlos Rodriguez."

"Oh, what! Did he suddenly remember where he left his car the night of the murder?" Dan made a scornful face.

"Well, as a matter of fact, he might have."

"What?"

"He's coming in with what he claims might be a very important piece of information with regard to Catherine Stevens' murder."

Dan looked at him with skepticism.

"I know." Bernie clenched his hand and went to look

The Secret Monster Within

for a stenographer.

***

Barry Shepherd chose to watch through the two-way mirror again as Dan and Bernie waited in the interrogation room. Carlos entered the room with his lawyer. "Here, sit down here, Dr. Rodriguez." Bernie indicated the chair he wished Carlos to sit on.

"And you can sit there, Mr. Flynn." He pointed to the chair upon which Carlos's lawyer was to sit.

They both obediently sat where indicated.

The court steno was already seated and ready to begin recording.

"You've been advised of all your rights?" Bernie looked at Carlos and his lawyer, knowing full well that they had.

They both nodded

"I'm sorry. You'll have to say yes or no so our stenographer can record it." Dan nodded his head at Lisa Barber who was already working the steno machine.

"Yes." They both responded together.

Bernie asked all the necessary questions pertaining to the identity of the one being interviewed so it would be on record. Then he took a deep breath and got into the meat of the interrogation.

"All right now. Let's start at the beginning." Bernie saw how uptight Carlos was and suggested he relax. "Could I get you some water?"

"Yes. Thank you."

Bernie called for a pitcher of water and some glasses.

"All right, Dr. Rodriguez. Tell us what happened the night you were called in to the hospital for an emergency. The night that Catherine Stevens was murdered."

Carlos wiped the sweat from his brow and looked at his attorney. Fred Flynn nodded his go-ahead.

"Ken Lopez is my cousin. On my mother's side," he added as an explanation for the different surnames. "We've been fairly close through the years. Ken is a good husband, a good father, and a good friend. He's been a member of the Lions for years and has done lots of charity work for them. He's been a devout Catholic all his life. He's always been a hard worker, and has provided well for his family."

Carlos sipped some of the water that had been provided, and then continued, "He has three children, two sons and a daughter, and ten grandchildren. In other words, he is one of the most upstanding and outstanding citizens you could find."

"That's why I couldn't tell you the truth the last time you had me in here. And why I'm finding it very difficult to do so now, because it just doesn't make any sense." Carlos shook his head and sipped more water.

"It's OK, Dr. Rodriguez. Do you mind if I call you Carlos?" Bernie asked softly.

"Oh, no. Carlos is fine."

"Thanks. Continue, please." Bernie leaned back in his chair in an effort to appear more relaxed. Dan followed his lead.

"Well," Carlos gave a nervous chuckle, "you've heard of the game Musical Chairs?"

"I guess we've all played that sometime in our lives." Bernie nodded.

"What I'm going to tell you is something like Musical Cars." Carlos tried to smile, but couldn't.

"Sounds interesting. Let's hear it." Bernie tried to keep it as low-keyed as possible. He could see the sweat beading Carlos Rodriguez's brow, and knew all the wiping in the world wouldn't make it go away.

The Secret Monster Within

"That night," Carlos continued, "when you questioned me about the whereabouts of my car, I told you I didn't know. When you told me it was at the waterfront, at the same time and place that Catherine Stevens was murdered, I couldn't believe it. I was so flabbergasted, I didn't know what to say."

"When you had determined that I had an airtight alibi, that I was, in fact, in the hospital when that girl was murdered, I figured I was off the hook. Let things lie as they were. You asked me if I had loaned my car to anyone that night, and I told you no."

Carlos looked at his lawyer once again. Fred Flynn nodded his encouragement.

"I lied."

"What?" Both Bernie and Dan sat up straight in their chairs at this remarkable news.

"I lied. I had loaned it to Ken Lopez, my cousin, this most gentle, sweetest man you could ever meet. I knew, I just knew, this murder couldn't have anything to do with him, so why get him involved? It had to be something else."

"Ken Lopez?" Bernie took a deep breath and tried to regain his cool.

"Yes. Ken. You've met him. You know him a bit. He helped lead that search through the woods for that twelve-year-old. Remember?"

"I remember it well," Bernie said.

"Well, you can see how ridiculous it all seemed to me when I heard my car was at the scene of the crime. Ken had my car, but he couldn't—he just couldn't have had anything to do with that." A tear escaped and trickled down the doctor's cheek. "He just couldn't," he said again. "That's why I lied."

"Tell us how he happened to have your car, Carlos.

Margaret McMillen

Start from the beginning." Bernie could feel his pain and decided the gentle approach was the proper one. Dan said nothing. No good cop bad cop needed for this interview. It was working just fine the way it was.

Chapter 42

Carlos dabbed at his sweaty brow and tear-stained cheek once more with his handkerchief.

"I can tell you what happened to the car that day. I can't tell you what happened that night." Carlos looked like a drowning man begging for a lifesaver.

"Go ahead, Carlos. Tell us about the car."

"Well," Carlos looked at his lawyer once more.

"Tell them everything, Carlos." Fred Flynn nodded his encouragement once more.

"OK. This is what happened. My cousin, Ken, and his wife, Maureen, were in a supermarket parking lot about a week before the night in question. They were just getting ready to leave when a car pulled in beside them. Without thinking or looking, the driver opened his car door and slammed it into the passenger side of Ken's car. It left a big dent, so they traded the usual information. Ken got three estimates as to the cost of the repairs for insurance purposes, and he opted to use Timothy's Collision Shop, since the price was right and he was promised it would be ready by the next day."

"You're doing fine, Carlos," Bernie said. "Just slow down a little bit so the stenographer can get it all." He smiled at the doctor.

"Oh, I'm sorry. I'm just so nervous."

"Understandable. Go ahead, Carlos."

Carlos took a deep breath and continued at a slower pace.

"Well, as it turned out, Timothy's Collision didn't have it done the next day, and that was the day of Ken's Lion's Club meeting. Ken is very proud of the fact that he hasn't missed a meeting in over thirty years, not even when he broke his leg. And, as it was, Maureen had already committed to do something that evening with her friends, so she needed her car. Out of desperation, Ken called me and asked if he could borrow my car for that night. As I've said, we've always been close."

Bernie nodded and indicated he should continue.

"I had no plans, so I figured, why not?" Carlos shrugged. "I told Ken that he was more than welcome to use my car. We don't live too far from each other, so he walked over and got it that very same day."

"I really should never do that because I am a doctor and have, on occasion, been called in for emergencies. But it's so rare." Carlos threw his hands up in an effort to emphasize the rareness of it. "Of course, as you now know, I *was* called in for an emergency. I'm a neurosurgeon, and a young fellow was brought in with a terrible head trauma resulting from a car accident that night, one that was a bit

The Secret Monster Within

too much for the young doctor on duty. Luckily, my wife had no plans for the evening, so I was able to use her car. It was her car that was parked in the parking ramp behind the hospital that evening, not my Lexus."

Carlos feared what that lie might cost him. Was this perjury? Could he be imprisoned? He didn't know what to expect.

"Well, Carlos," Bernie said, "you shouldn't have lied to us. You might have been able to save some lives if you had been truthful then. You do realize that, don't you?"

"Oh, God. Please don't let that be true. I don't think I can live with myself if that's true." Bernie and Dan could see the torment in Carlos' eyes. This was no acting job. He sincerely felt remorse. There was no doubt of that.

"You're a little late with this information, but we do appreciate that you finally found it in your heart to do the right thing. We know how hard it must be for you." Dan reached over and touched Carlo's arm.

"But you see, it's still all wrong." Carlos looked at Bernie and Dan and Fred, his eyes begging them to understand. "Kenny couldn't have done this horrible deed. You've got to find out what happened and how my car ended up at the scene of the crime." He squeezed his eyes shut in an effort to control the tears.

"Well, you know what? That is our job and we intend to do that very thing." Bernie rose and extended his hand to the doctor. "Thank you, Carlos. You may go now, and we'll be in touch. However, we must ask that you don't call Ken Lopez or contact him in any way until we do. You understand?"

"Of course," Fred Flynn said. "Mums the word till we hear from you. Right, Carlos?"

Carlos mumbled a barely discernable, "Right," as he shuffled out of the room, looking much older than he had when he came in.

Chapter 43

Ken and Maureen had just turned off the TV and were heading upstairs for bed when the doorbell rang.

"For heaven's sake. Who would be at the door at eleven o'clock at night?" Maureen was worried and it showed on her face.

"I'll check on it, honey. Stay where you are." Ken walked to the front door and looked through the peephole. There was a police car parked in front with two policemen standing on his front porch.

"Kenneth Lopez?"

He heard them call his name through the closed door.

"Yes?"

"Open the door, please."

The Secret Monster Within

"What's this all about?"

"We have a warrant for your arrest. Open the door, Lopez." The policeman's voice was booming.

"My arrest? What? This is some kind of joke. Right?"

Maureen came up to him. "What do they want, Ken?"

"They say I'm under arrest."

"What?" Maureen's face showed the shock she was feeling.

"What for?" she asked.

"I don't know. What's this for?" he shouted through the closed door.

"Open the damn door or we'll knock it in. Got it?" No more genial banter. The policemen were getting angry.

"How do I know you're policemen? This has got to be some kind of joke!"

"Well, we'll see just how funny you think it is. We can do this the easy way or we can do it the hard way. The hard way will cost you a brand new front door. You take your pick." The tall brawny cop was through being Mr. Nice Guy.

"Let me see proof of who you are," Ken demanded.

"Sure 'nuf. See?" The shorter cop showed his badge and opened his wallet so Ken could see his identification through the peephole.

It was either the best forgery in the world, or this pipsqueak was, indeed, an official police officer. Reluctantly, Ken opened the door.

The tall brawny cop grabbed him and pushed him into the room.

"What are you doing?" Ken was in a panic.

"Kenneth Lopez, you are under arrest for murder. You have the right to remain silent....." The little cop read him his rights.

"Ken! What's happening?" Maureen was beside herself.

"I don't know, honey. Call our lawyer and tell him what's happened. Have him meet me at the police station."

He saw her face contorted with fear. "It'll be all right, Maureen. This is just some kind of crazy mistake. Believe me!"

"Come on, sir." The smaller policeman escorted Ken down the front steps and into the squad car.

"Call Fred," Ken yelled to his wife just before he entered the car.

"I will, honey, right now." Maureen stood in a state of bewilderment as she watched the police car leave with her husband of so many years.

"This can't be happening," she said, as she entered her home to call their lawyer, Fred Flynn.

Fred answered on the first ring when he saw who was calling. He heard the panic in Maureen's voice and it was like a stab to his heart.

"Maureen," he said. "I know all about it."

"You know all about it? You know that Ken has been arrested? You know that they're saying he's wanted for murder?" She was almost hysterical.

"Yes, I do. I can't tell you how right now, but…" He couldn't find the words to explain what was happening. "Maureen, I don't know how to tell you this, but you're going to have to find another lawyer for Ken."

"Fred! Why? What are you saying? What's happening?" Maureen could barely speak through her sobs.

"Listen," Fred said, "I'll give you the name and number of a really good lawyer. Someone I know you can count on to do the best job possible."

"But Fred, you're our attorney. We don't want anyone else."

Fred took a deep breath before continuing. "Maureen,

you know that I've been Carlo's attorney even longer than I've been yours."

"What does Carlos have to do with this?"

"Oh, God. I don't know how to tell you this." He took another deep breath. "It seems that Carlos was brought in for questioning some time ago. The night that Catherine Stevens was murdered, someone saw a car parked nearby. He memorized the license plate number and reported it to the police. Maureen, the car was a blue Lexus, and it belonged to Carlos."

"What?" She fairly screamed it.

"I know. I know. As it turns out, Carlos knew something he didn't tell the police at that time."

He waited for her to respond, but there was dead silence.

"Maureen, that was the night he loaned his car to Ken. Carlos had an airtight alibi. He was at the hospital that night, the night that Catherine Stevens was murdered. But his car, the same blue Lexus he had loaned Ken, was at the scene of the crime."

"I don't understand."

"I know, Maureen. I wish there were an easier way to tell you all this. But I'm representing Carlos, so you can see why you have to have another lawyer—a good one—to take on Ken's case. I wish you all the best, but I can't help you."

There was no response.

"Maureen. Are you all right?"

Maureen answered weakly, "What do you think?"

Chapter 44

"Handcuffs?" Ken looked at the police officer as if he had gone mad. "I'm an upstanding citizen, a faithful churchgoer, a practicing Catholic, a husband, a father, a grandfather, and a member of the Lions. Do you think I'm going to cut and run?"

"I'm sorry, sir," the young policeman responded, and he looked as though he really meant it. "But it's regulations. I have to do this." He put the cuffs on Ken Lopez with his hands clasped in front.

"I hope no one's looking out their window," Ken said, as he was led from his house to the police car. "Thank God it's dark. This is most embarrassing."

"I can well imagine, sir." The policeman covered Ken's head with his hand as he helped ease him into the back seat of the patrol car.

It wasn't that far to the police station, although it felt more like a million miles. Ken looked this way and that, hoping no one would see him being escorted into the police station with his hands cuffed. Luckily, it was late and the area seemed devoid of any pedestrians.

"Right this way, sir." The arresting police officer indicated where Ken was to go. "We have to get your fingerprints first."

***

"Hello, Mr. Lopez." Bernie and Dan were waiting for him in the interrogation room.

"Have his rights been explained to him?" Bernie was looking at the arresting police officer.

"Most certainly, Chief Roper."

"Thanks, Kevin"

"I see you've been fingerprinted already, Mr. Lopez." Bernie had turned from Officer Newhouse and now glared at Ken Lopez.

"Yes. And I don't mind telling you that you've got a lot of explaining to do. My wife is on her way with our lawyer." At least Ken hoped so, though he didn't share his concern with Police Chief Roper. Maureen had been so distraught, he wasn't sure she could manage this simple task. He could only hope that Fred Flynn would be here soon.

"I also want you to know that I know my rights. I'm not saying a thing until my lawyer gets here. This is all ridiculous, and I'm sure that when he gets here, it will all be cleared up." Ken stuck his already prominent chin out in a display of strong fortitude.

"We understand. That is your right, Mr. Lopez. Could we get you a glass of water or anything while you're waiting?" Bernie was being most conciliatory.

"I could certainly use a glass of water. At least!" Ken rolled his eyes in disgust.

"Right you are." Bernie buzzed the intercom and asked for a glass of water.

It was close to an hour before Maureen arrived with a stranger in tow. She introduced her as Miss Jenelle Foster, Ken Lopez's lawyer. Maureen was told to wait in the lobby, while the flaming red-haired Miss Foster was escorted into the interrogation room.

Ken stared at the stranger with a big question mark on his face.

"Who are you?" he asked.

"It seems I'm your new lawyer," Jenelle Foster replied.

"What?"

"Your current lawyer, Mr. Fred Flynn, is representing Carlos Rodriguez. As you will see, this presents a conflict of interest. Mr. Flynn has had to bow out as your lawyer but he did pass on my name to your wife as someone to contact. So here I am, although I must confess, I know little of this case. Mrs. Lopez has tried to brief me, but she seems at a loss as to what is happening." She looked to Bernie and Dan.

Jenelle Foster was granted some necessary one-on-one time with her new client.

"Ken." Bernie was through with the proper salutation of Mister. As far as he was concerned, this was The Monster and he didn't merit any such polite address. He had all he could do not to sneer with revolt as he looked into Ken Lopez's bulging brown eyes.

"You do not deny that you borrowed Carlos Rodriguez's car the night that Catherine Stevens was murdered,

The Secret Monster Within

do you?"

Ken looked to his lawyer but was rewarded with nothing more than a shrug. A hell of a lot of good this woman's going to be. "No. I don't deny that. I did borrow Carlos's car that evening. I had a Lions meeting to go to and my car was in a collision shop being repaired."

"And you do know that Carlos Rodriguez's car was found parked at the waterfront, not far from the murder scene, don't you?" Bernie leaned forward and there was no hiding the feeling of repulsion he was experiencing.

"How the hell would I know that? He's not only my cousin, he's my friend as well. I needed a car that evening and he was kind enough to let me borrow his." Ken looked to his lawyer once more. "How it got to the waterfront I'll never know. But you can check. I was at the Lions Club meeting that night." His chin was jutting out even further.

"And what time did you get to the meeting, Ken?"

"I'm always there on time, seven o'clock. That's when the meeting starts."

"And what time is it over, Ken?"

Ken shrugged again. "It varies. But usually we're all gone by ten o'clock."

"And do you know when Catherine Stevens was strangled?"

Now Ken was showing signs of panic. "I remember reading it in the paper, but I don't recall it right now."

"Oh, really? Does 'somewhere between 10 PM and midnight ring a bell?"

Ken wiggled in his chair as his airtight alibi flew out the window. "Maybe." Again he looked to his lawyer who sat there like a wooden Indian.

"Well, you know what, Ken? Or should I say *Monster*? We've got your DNA off this glass." Bernie held up the water glass Ken had been using. "And, we've got the blood of The Monster on the willow branch that Sharon Kelly used to defend herself with when The Monster attacked her." Bernie enjoyed watching Ken Lopez squirm. "How much do you want to bet they match?"

"For Chrisakes, do something!" Ken was yelling at his lawyer.

Chapter 45

"No way!" Jennifer stared at the TV with open mouth. "Vince, did you hear that?"

Vince was shaking his head. "It can't be," he said.

"Mr. Lopez? The Monster? Good Lord. What if it's really true? When I think of the number of times my family and I have been together with him." She gasped as another thought occurred to her. "Oh, my God. I was alone with him at Playground for Kids when he came in to sign up his granddaughter. Melanie wasn't there that day. He actually warned me then about my chances of becoming a victim because I was young, short and brunette." Jennifer shivered at the thought of what might have been. "Is that weird or not?"

"Weird isn't the word for it. He seems so nice." Vince was incredulous.

"I know. I still find it too hard to believe. But they say the DNA of the blood on the willow branch and that of Ken Lopez is a perfect match. And the car he borrowed that evening was at the scene of the crime. I can't see any other explanation. Can you?"

Again Vince shook his head. "No, I can't."

Melody's cry brought them back to the present. Jen ran to the nursery and reached for her crying baby. She hugged her to her breast and kissed the top of her head. The wispy softness of the blue-black curls always brought her joy, but today she shivered.

"Melody, my dear sweet baby. He might have killed me, and then there would be no you." The thought was overwhelming and brought her to tears.

***

There was no fighting the DNA. It was a perfect match.

"Why did you do it?" Bernie asked. "You had the perfect life. You're well off, you have a lovely family, and you are respected in the community. I mean, you have everything that most people wish for. Why would you do such horrible, despicable acts of violence against all these young girls? Why, Ken?"

"I didn't. The Monster did." Ken Lopez looked as though he was going to cry.

"The Monster? That's what the media called you even before we knew whom you were. Why are you claiming him now?"

Because when I read about it and they gave him that name, I knew that's exactly who it was that resided inside me. It was a Monster. And the Monster's not *me*."

"All right, Ken. We know who you are. Who is The Monster?"

The Secret Monster Within

"He killed my sister and my mother. And now, all these girls."

"Your sister and your mother?" Bernie looked at Dan with a look of bewilderment.

"Yes." Now the tears were flowing freely down Ken Lopez's cheeks.

"I loved my mother dearly." Ken's eyes went dreamy. "More than I can say. She and I were very close. In fact, she nursed me until I was almost six years old."

Again, Bernie and Dan exchanged looks but said nothing.

"I know now that most women don't do that, but I didn't know that then." Ken looked for some understanding in either cop's eyes, but found none.

"But then my mother became pregnant and had a baby girl. Suddenly, I was no longer welcome to nurse at my mother's bosom. Now it was only for my sister. I hated her." Again Ken looked at both cops and they could see the poison spewing from his eyes. "My sister, I mean," Ken went on to explain.

"She had taken my place. My mother was still nice to me, but not like she used to be before Jeanine was born. I detested my little sister. Who was she to take my mother's love and affection and time from me?"

"It was then, for the very first time, that I got to know The Monster."

"Go on, Ken." Bernie spoke softly.

"One night, when everyone was asleep, The Monster told me to get out of bed and go into my sister's room. I did what he told me. She was sleeping on her back, so it was really very easy. All I had to do was take the pillow he had told me to bring and cover her sweet little face. It wasn't long before she had gone to live with the angels." Ken smiled as he remembered it.

"The Monster was my friend, you see. He had fixed the problem."

"What happened after that, Ken?" Bernie had all he could do to keep his voice on an even keel.

"Well, it didn't work like it was supposed to. My mother went into a fit of depression. She thought the baby had died of Sudden Death Syndrome, and she was devastated. Suddenly, she would have nothing to do with me. She wouldn't even talk to me. Eventually, they had to put her in a psychiatric ward at the hospital." Ken was sobbing now.

"She killed herself while there. I never saw her again."

"So The Monster wasn't your friend after all?" Bernie was confused.

"Well, he didn't seem to be at the time, but I knew in my heart he had tried to help me. It just didn't work out. He became my friend again years later."

"You mean when you started killing the young ladies in Buffalo and then in Amherst?" Dan had been quiet up till now.

"Yes. That's when he came back to me. He told me I needed a reason for my mother's death. Why did my mother do this to me? The guilt and the sorrow I was feeling were all her fault."

Bernie and Dan stared at this being but didn't say a word.

"She was in her late twenties when she died. She was short and had dark curly hair. She had caused me so much pain by what she did that I had to kill her again and again. The Monster told me to."

"Ken. Is that why every one of your murder victims had a red X mark across the nipple of each breast?" The signature act of The Monster was now making more sense. Bernie knew the answer even before he asked the question.

The Secret Monster Within

"Yes." He nodded vigorously. "She wouldn't let me suckle any more, even after my sister was gone. She had to pay for that again and again."

"Through the deaths of these young girls you didn't even know?" Bernie had all he could do to control himself.

"I know how wrong it was of The Monster to do these horrible crimes. I wish I could have found some way to relieve myself of him." Ken was sobbing uncontrollably, but he elicited no feelings of sympathy from Bernie or Dan. It was all they could do to keep themselves under control.

"Ken," Dan said, "tell us why you did a rash of them in Buffalo, and then went years with no killings. And why then did you start again in Amherst?"

"That's easy to explain," Ken said. "When we were first married, Maureen and I lived in a house across the street and two doors away from my parents' house. Every day I saw it and it was a reminder of my mother and what she had done to me. The hate grew and festered and that's when The Monster started his killing spree. That lasted for a relatively short time, as you know. Then my father loaned me some money and I started a new business. Within three years, it was successful and not long after, my wife and I decided to move. We bought a home in Amherst." Ken saw the stenographer racing to catch his every word.

"It was a new beginning. We had a new home far away from the one that had so many bad memories. The Monster regressed. He was under control and I had a good life. I was happy to be rid of him, the Monster, I mean."

"And then I met Jennifer Wilkins. She reminded me so much of my mother that, in spite of the blue eyes, The Monster returned. He made me do it, you know. I had no control."

Dan and Bernie exchanged glances.

"Why didn't you go after this Jennifer Wilkins then,

Ken?" Dan asked what all in the room were wondering.

"Because I loved her. And I loved her family. It was a war between The Monster and me. He wanted me to kill her. He kept insisting on it, but I hoped if I gave him someone else, he would let me off the hook. So I gave him one after another." Ken closed his eyes and shook his head. "And still he wasn't satisfied. Nothing would satisfy him until I killed Jen. I knew in my heart that I had to kill her. It would be the only way to stop all these other killings. One life lost for so many saved. But I just couldn't do it. I loved her like a daughter."

"Can you see my dilemma?" Ken looked to Bernie and Dan for empathy, but received none. They knew this man was insane, but neither could hide the loathing he felt for him.

***

"I'm guilty." Ken Lopez's chin no longer stood out in a sign of defiance. Rather, it lay upon his chest in a manner of defeat as he looked at the judge with soulful eyes. There was no fighting the DNA. His lawyer had pled insanity, although neither he nor anyone else expected much mercy from the court for this monstrous killer. And there was none to be had.

There was no doubt that Ken Lopez was insane, and the judge ordered him to be held in a psychiatric center where he was to remain for life. If, per chance, he should ever be considered sane in the future, then he was ordered to spend the rest of his life in prison with no chance of parole

And now it seemed The Monster was finally gone.

Epilogue

Maureen Lopez stood by her husband until she heard the whole sordid story. This was a man she had loved and lived with for over forty years, and yet he was more a stranger to her now than anyone she was likely to meet. He had cried and begged forgiveness, but how could she forgive the horrible deeds he had done? How could she ever forgive or forget them? Within a year, she had sold their business and sought an annulment.

For the first year, Kyle and Rachel still came back to Buffalo to visit Maureen for frequent visits, but when her sons opted to move out west where their name did not bear the stigma it had in the Buffalo area, Maureen chose to move also. Ken Lopez would never see any of his family again.

***

For some unknown reason, Ken Lopez would not confess to the murder of Barbara Fairchild, and he repeatedly denied knowing where her body was. The police knew better and begged him to tell Barbara's family so they might recover the body and receive some closure, but he steadfastly refused. Neither Bernie nor Dan could understand his reason for denying this one murder when he had already confessed to so many others, but they guessed it might have something to do with the victim's very young age. Whatever the reason, there would be no closure for the family of Barbara Fairchild.

***

Sharon Kelly reveled in the fact that The Monster had been finally caught and was behind bars. She started eating and sleeping again, and her career took an upward swing. She felt reborn and she knew her life had just begun.

So many lives had been lost, but hers was new again.

***

And Jen Wilkins would never know how close she had come to being the prime victim of The Monster.

CPSIA information can be obtained
at www.ICGtesting.com
Printed in the USA
BVOW03s1819151117
500518BV00001B/8/P